Victorious Delusions

A Tale of the Late 1960's

By

Victor E. Navarro, Jr.

To Adrienne,
Victor

Best of luck in your
painting & college work.
Best wishes always,
Victor E Navarro, Jr.

© 2002 by Victor E. Navarro, Jr. All rights reserved.

No part of this book may be reproduced, stored in a retrieval system, or transmitted by any means, electronic, mechanical, photocopying, recording, or otherwise, without written permission from the author.

ISBN: 1-4033-8481-9 (e-book)
ISBN: 1-4033-8482-7 (Paperback)
ISBN: 1-4033-8483-5 (Hardcover)

Library of Congress Control Number: 2002095730

This book is printed on acid free paper.

Printed in the United States of America
Bloomington, IN

1stBooks – rev. 01/22/03

Preview to Victorious Delusions © 2002, a poem by Victor E. Navarro, Jr.

It seemed that abstract art
Would enter in the sixties
But it never sustained the
Blow Mr. Kuput gave it
Although he sort of liked it.

Long golden hair approached me
As I went to the campus of legibility
With sayings written on the walls
Of the Fine Arts complex,
A life Hitler may have lived,
I thought, without taking one
Amphetamine, if that's possible
For an artist—even in January I sped
At Dead Man's Hill with a sled
To roll down forever the projected
Memories from those times I knew
Better than anything.

A vision or two appeared
In sleep as the March winds
Swirled over the city, where
I lost my mind's eye one night

On the Ide's perhaps.
How many times would I be there?
And in the sun I swept away
All traces of the gloom—from
That first Lucky to the first Lark
Was five years of poetry.
And zoos came forward
In animalistic rhythms
As if there were more who
Could refute the testimony
Of those who doubted realism.

To her who wanted money
Instead of a friend in need
Of some reward for a lost penny
Of a dream, I took a voyage to the
Seashore, and saw Rosemary from the
Sands, talking to a stud who didn't
Like me from the first. How could a
Journey start there?

In the depths of philosophical investigation
I watched the lions sleep in their cells of
Iron and cement, never guessing that I went
With them to sleep each night in a Highland

Park site not far from the East River.

Christmas Eve always came soon enough
To solace my love's lost heart without fanfare.

I once vanished for nights on end
As a Johnny Carson fan, perhaps
Not staged for anyone except my aunt.
I can't accept the following of a guru
From across the ocean.

Pure forms of nature were what I
Worshipped, occasionally at the dusk
Of a Fox Chapel road wondering who
Was driving the car that spun through
The roads in the dark.

Mr. Kuput once said that all visions
Have luck, and it made me say back to him—
Fuck.

ACKNOWLEDGEMENTS

I deeply thank the following persons for their encouragement and assistance during the years of my writing this novel: my cousin, Nellita Link, and her husband, Tom Link, of Pittsburgh, Pennsylvania; my cousin, Tom Moore, Jr., of Miami, Florida, who transcribed my handwritten manuscript onto electronic disks; and Rosemary Garcia- Pendleton, Library Director, Miami-Dade Community College, Homestead Campus, for her research.

Victorious Delusions
A Tale of the Late 1960's

PART I—1967

Victor E. Navarro, Jr.

Prelude

There were times when all seemed in light—the shade was gone, rearranged by the sun and in it more light than a thousand stars. This was in the past when I knew people, people who saw themselves as gods bent on doing something, anything that would seem creative or even artistic. But this was a long time ago and out of those shadows came real forces of things yet to be discovered. What made that past so beautiful was its flow. It flowed on and on as the wind on an October afternoon glides through the yellow-leafed trees. In the Fall for some reason or other (I don't quite know as yet) was the time for all these events to happen. Other seasons had their own special glory but the Fall seemed to be the premier season of them all. Perhaps it was the weather that made it that way. Anyway, the past was huge in its flowing dimensions and released something that let the calm winds blow steadily forward giving life to the newborn ideas that emerged with the hippie era of the middle sixties. This era had been born alone, a stranger to the other eras.

Down into the past, way down into the past I explored a region of space that called itself by no name. It was a quiet place, far from the apartments and pads of the hippies who inhabited that part of town. Where we would go for the night was the major topic of that era and there were times when all we would do would be to loaf at the local college. Then, of course, there was the coffee house on a side street in a colorful part of town. There we would join each other for poetry and guitar playing until midnight. Then we would go for some pizza or perhaps a hamburger until our faces were stuffed. What greater times from afterwards when, finished eating, there were nights of grass and speed and sometimes acid when getting stoned was the order of the times. I remember those nights well and how we would look for girls to share our time with. They were sexual times and filled with a peace not yet discovered since then.

Memories of Annie in the Spring of 1967

Spring came in with flair. The warm days were plentiful and the warm breezes ran into you as you walked outside. The hills were still bare and they stood there unaware of the warm weather. It was mid April. My walks had not been too proficient these days and I didn't walk much at all in the hot spell we had in the middle of April. It was in the eighties for several days and a cooling trend was not in sight. I had not decided on a walk for that Friday. The weekend was here and all the trimmings that go with it arrived on time making this Friday a special day. I had hoped to make every day a special day in my life thus duplicating the process of living in two eras—the past and the future. The past was filled with memories of other Springs when I was younger and more adventurous. The adventures of past Springs came forward like the burst of warmth had come unheralded by any sign yet sure enough arrived in the past few days. That past which hung about my memory like a vise enclosed everything within it. The old days were as new – again and again they came back, reflected upon in a new light. It was as if the whole era of the past days shone forth without relapse and again came back, reflected upon, in a new light, coming into my mind wherever I went, always here, always beckoning me forward to grasp its unusual trends. The past had lived itself right up to the present and had gained in its intensity over the years to make a sure thing surer in light of all the things I had done in those past days. The past shaped all things new and exhibited the larger share of activities which were to be done in the next few weeks. All of this seemed new to me as I groped into that past with a fine-toothed comb. Separating the memories was not difficult and consumed little time so that I was aware of the old ages in my mind slowly taking form again in the present and relieving everything around me so as to give a feeling of worth to all the things I presently was doing. The past was recaptured again and again giving a sense of reality which gave no clue to its underpinnings yet was so effective in its sweep of time. So dear to me were those memories that lingered on and on never stopping for an instant but ever-present and aware of the times which had gone by. All of the streams of consciousness gave themselves to my heart and revealed the past in all its shining glory. There were times when I would awake half-dazed, half naked of the past's revealings that were so true and so beautiful as to make the day seem real once again in my eyes. There were many times when I would think of the people of the past with feeling and love knowing that they were gone forever yet shielding them from that loss, so dear were they to my soul. I went along slowly at first and then more rapidly in transcribing those events and characters to fill the void of present days.

Annie must be made real again for me to function well, and her fragrance must come back to me on warm Spring days in the sun just as she used to warm me in April of 1967 when all was a calm adventure into the nights and again into the days of that April.

I remember George H., too, and how he used to swing onto the street with his "mod" clothes and record album tucked under his arm. He was a stalwart loafer back in those days. But Annie was the main thing back in that Spring. She and I were in love in an odd kind of way and though we had a good relationship we saw each other almost every night that April and we went out together a lot on those balmy nights way back in the past. Back in the past everything leads from those days and everything intersects at a point not far from a lovely day in April, 1967 when Annie and I would meet in Shadyside to take "speed" together on Walnut Street with all the other freaks there. Annie enjoyed speed in a great fashion and she and I kept several bottles on hand for our speed trips. Dexedrine was what we had the most bottles of and we would take about three or four capsules to start off the night. Annie was really into her painting then and she would paint while on speed for hours at a time, never stopping except to light a cigarette or to play with her pet rabbits. Annie looked so beautiful to me on speed that I used to picture her as a street whore, all gaudy and ready for the catch. She and I went everywhere together at night but saw little of each other during the day (except when she would stay up all night speeding and we would be with each other the next day). Of course, she had her art classes in the daytime too, which took up most of the days. But at night it was a different story. We went to the Rising Tide several times on Saturday nights. We went into town and spent a lot of time on Walnut Street. Annie is gone now but her memory still stays in my mind as if it all happened yesterday. It is funny how the past creeps up on us and bends us into its will. The past I knew in those days of April 1967, is still alive and vibrant, surging forth in a new way, always present in my memory like an event which is impossible to forget. All that time in between yet Annie still lives! What is there to have forgotten about those times? Nothing, really, and yet the days flow onward, rolling against each other, showing the way for the future to bring its heralded times forward. The past which Annie and I had is too proven a stimulant for better days ahead. If that past cannot be repeated at least it can be remembered with a cherished silence like all good memories have attached to them. In this silence Annie comes and goes revealing all of herself to me once again as I traverse those same paths which we took years ago. In recapturing that past with Annie I have reseen a new heaven which gives me new pleasures far removed from the old ones I once had. This new era of nostalgia and remembrance gives me almost the same pleasures that the original era gave me. How far removed we are from reality when we recapture lost times and bring those times to life again. A new reality sets in and gives us light and peace to replace the old times we once knew.

On Annie and George H.

To put Annie on paper doesn't do justice to her flowing blond hair in the April winds of 1967. Annie was a fully developed character, not of some book, but of the book of life. My experiences with her were various and she was always with me or in my mind during those times. I have written at length about her in THE LOAFING PAPERS and this presents a complete picture of her and her habitat during the Spring of 1967. That Spring was one of a kind and the elements that comprised it were evidently tantamount to the times themselves. That Spring had other characters in it also, such as Arthur R. and George H. Arthur was my Winter companion before I met Annie and he and I shared a lot together including our tastes for literature and speed. We took speed together a lot that winter and we stayed up all night together many times reading or watching late movies (especially the old Bogart films as well as Cagney and John Wayne).

Once in awhile Nancy L. would join us for an all-nighter and she fit into the program quite nicely with her long brown hair and blue eyes. Arthur played the role of our son when Nancy was with us. Arthur fit well into the role of the child. He played up to Nancy and myself and he was never at a loss for a pithy comment or antic. George H. also figured to be a factor in the late Spring after I didn't see Annie as much as I used to. It was in May that George H. appeared on the scene of my life. He filled in the tapestry quite well with his dealership in grass and acid. He was well known on Walnut Street and would show off his social talents quite a bit, especially when dealing in acid (which he liked to take a lot of). To say that George H. was a main character of the sixties is to put him too mildly into perspective. He was a major character indeed. His antics were unequaled in the annals of the sixties. He was a major force on Walnut Street and for the acid-hippie he was the dealer extraordinaire. Dressed to the hilt in his mod clothes he always had a good thing to say about someone or other and he never let you forget who got you all that grass and acid. He used to prance along Walnut Street and he walked tall with all the hippies who loafed on the street back in those lost days of 1967.

The Spring of 1967

To say that Annie belonged to the past is to say that she was a creature of the past. The past nourished and fed her and it gave her a fragrance of lost lilies in some forgotten chamber. Annie had all the makings of a truly marriageable girl and she forgot about time when she was with me. That is, she never counted the hours when she was with me but strung along hopefully until we would finish our nightly stint together. Annie had no trouble with words and would use them with great charm as she headed out for an evening in that Spring of

Springs in 1967. All eras lead to that Spring just as they all converge from it as a focal point of the past, never relapsing into a forgetfulness of things that were and were to be. Those times came and went, to be sure, all too quickly, but they left their mark on the history of things in general. The Spring of 1967 was shaped and reshaped of the happenings of those days, all too frequently lost in the endless pages of the past. It was a short time that Annie and I spent together but it was an intense time, filled with all the happenings of a love affair mixed with drug addiction and commonly spelled-out mechanisms of nostalgia which gave the times a flavor far removed from the ordinary and just as intricate. Annie was always on my mind in those days and she was reborn every day in that Spring just as the plants and trees were reborn for the year. Annie played in the sun like a little girl and it is that little girl quality that remains foremost in my memory. Listening to Donovan and going with Annie were two things that I did in that Spring. It was the best Spring by far that I ever had. There was such a peacefulness to it that it brought forth creative energies never before or since equaled. The times make the man and I would say that the Spring of 1967 made me a whole person, complete with a repertoire all my own. It gave me confidence for future eras and it made me aware of all the possibilities of life in all its inherent glory. Those times are gone now, but they remain embedded in a stream bed far away from the shore yet so close to the woods.

Victorious Delusions
A Tale of the Late 1960's

Annie and the Lost Days

The sound of wheels on the pavement—I feel the wheels crush against the street as I walk down the hill towards the store to get a newspaper—the cars whiz by me as I shift and make the turn to another street that leads to the store —wheels screeching as a car turns at the corner, tires made bald by the driving habits of the car's owner—the long walk back from the store up the hill—I reach the house and pull my key from my pocket.

It's a sunny day today. It is in early May and the trees have started getting green as the warm winds of Summer begin to appear. A walk to the zoo I plan for later in the day. There should be animals outside today, especially the rhinoceros which roams in his area alone with the wind. But the wind is calm today. A thousand smiles issue from the passers-by as they walk up to the park.

Annie would have loved it all. She would have danced in the sun, overjoyed to go to the zoo for she was an artist and she drew animals for study in art. Her paintings were excellent. She combined her colors smoothly and she presented her images with professionalism and charm.

But she is gone now and that is another story. Her departure left me cold and lonely and I missed her deeply during those times. We had some good times together, we played together often during that Spring that we spent with each other. We used to get soft ice cream together on warm evenings. The Spring we spent together was a warm one especially in April and May. It seemed that Summer would come early that year. The trees were green on the first of May and the bushes were lush by that time. Annie was working on a painting entitled "King of Hearts" and she worked at it voraciously from the morning until late at night. Those lost days come back to me sometimes. They come in the morning, afternoon, and once in awhile in the evening. How can one recapture those lost days? It's not easy. You have to be in the right frame of mind. Also you have to be receptive to the vibrations of the past which come from viewing in the present the old places where you used to hang out in the past. The old places are the foundation on which to build your recapture of the past. The past flows freely from these old places and you can see the past once again when you are in the spell of the old places. Old places such as Annie's old apartment building bring back memories of Annie when I used to visit her there. Also the old places contain a nostalgia which is unequaled by meditation or reflection on the past. The past can be recaptured best from those old places where it all once happened years ago in a day filled with brighter sunshine than these present days are. In the old days things happened more quickly and more persistently than in the present days. In the old days things were more intense and took on more meaning. The way Annie used to meet me at night in April and May of 1967 was different from the way I see each night come in the present. Speed and acid added an original flavor to the old days which is missing from the present days.

Victorious Delusions
A Tale of the Late 1960's

Where are those lost days that used to seem so real and so alive with adventure. They are buried, I guess, in the past never to be seen again except in the memory. There are times when those lost days reappear before my mind in all their splendor. The forgotten dreams of the past lie buried in our brains waiting for the chance to be reborn with a flash of reminiscence. I lost Annie somewhere in that past and yet Annie still lives on in my memory. The lost Annie comes to me again on warm Spring days. She is rediscovered through my memory of her soft golden hair flowing in the sun. I can still picture her by my side during the night, creeping around (the two of us), waiting for the speed to take effect. The speed would last long once it hit you and the high was glorious and true to the mark. We would stay up all night speeding our brains out, laughing at the night, and daring it not to smoothly continue into daylight—the morning coming all too soon to our sides, never beckoning us towards it, but slowly wending its way to our eyes as sleep had left us alone that night. The highlights of a speed high are usually the creativity that the high enables. Painting and writing, Annie and I would spend our speed nights creating forms that were lasting in themselves, showing no sign of loss or failure, and giving all the warmth of life to its creators as a mask that covers the night with blue and green shades intermingled with poetry and non-fiction too. How we used to create on speed! Annie had her painting to do and she did it well on speed. She developed a love for speed that had no other equal. Her dependence on the drug was evident from the start and she took it in large doses to keep her awake and high all through the night. Annie took speed with a passion and she waited eagerly for the next speed high as if she were waiting for a big event in her life. She also liked to rap on speed with me and she liked to fuck on speed too. She fucked real good on speed and kissed with a great passion while high on the drug. So the lost days return, remembering the speed highs with Annie and the warm Spring nights we spent together.

I thought of the plane Elaine would be flying back in and I hoped it would be a safe flight for her. I was afraid myself of planes. I liked trains and always took them when I went to New York City. She was coming back at last! The dreams I had of the return could now come true for me as I lay on my sofa and thought of her and her looks. Annie never made such a lovely picture and I could recapture all of our times together with a moment's trip to my memory, which functioned well then and I was accustomed to changes in it from the earliest days of remembrance of things past which occurred in the mid-sixties when I was seeing Laura as I saw her many times back in those days by the Syria Mosque where I would sit sometimes in between classes and think of past eras. My remembrance of the past began in that era of the Mosque steps and continued ever since as a projection of myself unannounced but always in process. My memory formed a tapestry of images which were centered around the sixties —the time of my teens—and there were many different eras to choose from to remember with a beautiful nostalgia all their own. I once discussed this with Arthur, who seemed angered at my pastime as well as my past as I related events from lost eras to him one night while on speed in January of 1967. Annie was not there that night. It was just Arthur and I. Forgotten were the days of high school though I still remembered pastiches of those days in the sunlight of a summer in late August of 1969 during a break in a depression that began with the Spring and didn't end until 1970. Then there was the age of the "roach" and Ed's new place with his mother and her boyfriend who was a big drunk and quite nasty wth Ed's friends though I felt bad for him because he was crippled. Arthur and I spoke at length that night on speed about the past and Arthur said that he was thinking of writing a novel about the past and its stains. To my knowledge he never wrote the novel or even began to write it but he had all the ideas for it down pat. I thought of Arthur as I waited for Elaine and I knew that he was somewhere showing off his ass to the society which he frequented. That was Arthur. He was so unlike Uncle Art even though they both had the same name, but I never remembered them in one image together. They were always separated in my mind as if born to be that way for a good reason. Arthur could have brought out Art's image, I knew that. But they were from different eras altogether and didn't share the same way of thinking.

And so Elaine was to return at the onset of Fall. I was prepared for her arrival even though it was to be a month or more away. I put most of my books upstairs away from me, but left Proust's A *l'ombre des jeunes filles en fleurs* (Within a Budding Grove) and a History of

Mathematics downstairs where I could get to them. I was busy with the piano, especially Old English music which I just purchased.

There were many days that Elaine and I spent looking at different parts of the city. We would travel all around town searching for little cafes and diners where we could shop and have coffee or a sandwich. Some of the time we brought Mr. Kuput along with us, but for the most part it was just the two of us. We had much fun doing this and it lasted through October and into the first half of November. By then the leaves changed and the world around us was filled with brilliant colors. The really cold weather was not here yet and it was still a good time for walks in various parts of the city. Elaine, the romanticist, would sometimes hold my hand on some walks just as she used to do when I first met her at college years before. It was such a peaceful time for both of us but we agreed as to its meaning for each of us. It seemed to me so much better than the speed-inflated days with Annie that I stopped referring to them in my writings and began to concentrate on the days that I had with Elaine. I thought Elaine was so much prettier than Annie that it was stupid to compare them to each other. I loved the Fall in those days and especially I loved the emergence of winter in November.

Years before I did a painting of a mountain in late November and I thought of how it just might be my favorite time of year. The walks through the parks became a daily routine for us and we passed by the scenes more quickly than we used to. The happiness that a certain thing evokes can be measured by the time you spend doing that. We spent a lot of time in the parks that Fall and I can still remember Elaine's camel-lined jacket that she wore that was a bit short at the sleeves but kept her warm on cool mornings and afternoons and evenings when we went walking. When I was not with her I would take long walks alone, perhaps to Squirrel Hill, perhaps to one of the parks. Once in awhile I drove to the country alone but mostly I stayed in the city where I found all that I needed to inspire me to keep me going.

My writing was coming along more prolifically and I was trying to get the feel of a certain style which I believed to be caused by Elaine because she inspired me as much to create beauty as beautiful as she was beautiful with her whitish blond hair blowing in the cool autumn wind that became an integral part of my dreams. I find it difficult to assess the state of my dreams in that dreams were mere happenings that burst forth from the night during sleep. I didn't analyze much during that time and I gained an awareness that reflected the peaceful adventures I was having, so many adventures they were, though simple ones with no true excitement except the joy of living, that I last had of them when I sat down to write about something in the late night when I would get home from seeing Elaine. My brain processes were not limited however to the brief notes I took but spread to past days as well as to the core of the adventures I was having with her in that favorite time of year when things are so calm that you would think them to be frozen in space and time. We soon lost track of Mr. Kuput and we were not to see him again until Christmas time. But we didn't miss him at all and I regarded him then as I regarded Arthur, as an eccentric who would not really care if he were avoided for whatever the reason. After all, I thought, Mr. Kuput had things he wanted to get done and he deserved some time to himself. Elaine was all I cared about during those days of love and quiet. Such quiet it was! I saw fields of pure grass in the winds of November as we walked through the trail in the park I liked best. The trees were becoming bare and the grass stopped growing due to the new cold that emerged in the middle of the month. No warm spells would come -that was fine with the two of us as we progressed our way towards Winter and a new era that we said would be even greater than the one we were both sharing then. But the Winter was a way away and we decided to take even longer walks that Thanksgiving when we were going to Cd's farm for that holiday. We looked forward to that day because we loved his farm as we had enjoyed many parties there over the years. Mildred was having a party soon and we would be going to it. Elaine didn't want to bring along Kuput to that party and I agreed with her though it was originally my idea to bring him there. He didn't know Mildred and he was so critical!

That November was the end point of some writing Elaine was doing and she began typing her results.

Lost days were revived as Crazy Bob entered the picture with his special brand of advice and philosophy. Elaine knew him from college days when he used to hang out at the campus student union and other places on campus. He was quite a stalwart force in those days and he still went there once in awhile though I had not seem him there in years. When I saw him he told me he wanted to hang out with me and Elaine "like old times." I told him "ok" and we arranged to meet at the scene on a Saturday night around nine o' clock. I hoped Elaine would go along with the idea though I wasn't sure she would. She once told me that she wasn't fond of Crazy Bob because he once tried to rape her while she was a junior in college. He claimed to have slept with her but she told me it wasn't true and I believed her rather than him because he was so full of stories that once you knew him it was hard to believe all that he said. I called Elaine that evening and she agreed to come with me to the scene to meet Crazy Bob. It seemed a new era was developing along the lines of an old era. So many memories came to mind about him that I couldn't digest them all.

And I remained skeptical about the result of this new surge of interest in Elaine and me on Bob's part. But that Saturday evening came and it was a surprise to say the least. Bob was full of energy that night and we three had a good conversation—and when we left for our respective houses Bob made arrangements to meet us at the college campus snack bar the next Monday evening. I was looking forward to this because Bob knew many of the students there and I wanted to see if he acted differently there than he did at the coffeehouse with just Elaine and me present. That Sunday, Elaine and I went to a museum with Mr. Kuput and we asked him to join us

Monday but he declined because he had another engagement. All the same I still wanted Bob to meet Mr. Kuput some day, probably at the campus. My goal for this meeting was sometimes before Christmas and I was sure he would hit it off with Bob as Bob was as grand a loafer as Mr. Kuput. Elaine and I slept together that Sunday night and I felt relieved to know that she still had desires for me even though she was quite lax in her attentions and affections that night. We went on like this for several months until the holiday season when things changed abruptly.

Elaine and I got along well during that time of Crazy Bob's beginning of a new era with us. In a way it was good to have him back even though he still went about with his usual antics like talking about psychology in which neither Elaine nor I were really interested. But aside from that he was quite a bit of fun. Bob liked to ride sleds and disks down Flagstaff Hill or even in King's Estates. We never tried Dead Man's Hill but we hoped to try it that Winter. Dead Man's Hill was very steep though I used to ride it often when I was young. Elaine had never ridden it. Neither had Bob. Winter was just a month away and you could feel it slowly emerging in the November air.

So my search for Crazy Bob ended and with the end of the search came a new era of adventures at the college campus. He especially liked Science Hall, which had its own little automated snack area with sandwiches and drinks. There was never any one in that area so we could go there for a drink and talk and sometimes use the computers in the computer room. Bob shared someone's password he got on the computer and we could write our own programs into the thing. It was interesting once in awhile. We also went to the Fine Arts Building where we played the pianos and listened to a student's recital. They also put on plays which we sometimes attended. Bob always had a comment for the recitals and the plays but Elaine enjoyed them immensely. The nights were getting longer and flurries of snow fell once during that November. I never thought of Annie in the Fall except for the last time I saw her which was in that season, and I thought of that occasion more than once. Ellen and Karen were Fall memories for me as well as George H., the Dude, and Ed and the old clique of 1969. Except for the Dude I never saw any of them because I had Elaine and now Crazy Bob again. The new adventures were just as pleasing as the old ones. My hours were about the same except that the people in them changed. Elaine, because she was a few years younger than I, didn't have many past eras to think about—that was perhaps why she seemed so much more alive than I did to myself. Or perhaps it was my imagination that saw all of this.

One night Elaine and I met Crazy Bob at the Open Pantry and then, after coffee, we went to Crazy Park to smoke some cigarettes. It was cool but not as cool as the Open Pantry where freaks came at all times of the year for coffee and hot chocolate in the Fall and Winter and for cokes and iced tea in the Spring and Summer. Freaks of all kinds would hop in and out of the place at all hours of the night. It was the most famous way station except for the scene and the campus. Bob turned me on to it years before and Elaine and I stopped there on our way to and from the park when we walked in that particular park. Ever since Weinstein's burned down I remember going to the Open Pantry. We sat in Crazy Park for several hours and then we walked to Squirrel Hill which was not far away and Bob went to his home while I walked Elaine home and then walked all the way to my house. I felt excited about being alone that night for a weird reason. I felt more free than when I was with Bob and Elaine. It was my days alone that I remembered during that time. They were so peaceful yet so lovely. After I got home I read and then wrote a little and went to sleep more quickly than I had in a long time. The walk had made me tired. The next day we didn't see Bob at all but we had an adventure in Schenley Park near the oval and in the woods. It was a sunny Fall day and we were stimulated by the beauty of that day. Elaine mentioned Mr. Kuput but I changed the subject because I knew Mr. Kuput was busy with work even though he was retired. He would work occasionally for stretches, he told me. We watched some people playing tennis and then we drove to the edge of the city to look at houses we admired. I was critical of some of the homes but Elaine liked them all. We talked of the house we would one day get for ourselves. It was a hopeful day for both of us. We went out for dinner and then retired early, planning to meet the next day for another sojourn in one of the city parks. I listened to classical music on the radio that night and didn't get to sleep until after four though I didn't read or write at all. The nights were indeed getting longer, I thought, as I got into bed and shut out the light. I would see Elaine again tomorrow.

They called Crazy Park by that name because of all the acid and speed that had been taken there in the past. There was a frantic sort of aura to the park. Several paths led into thick woods, where children would ride the swings and play on the monkey bars. The boulevard passed close by the edge of the park where the swings were. It wasn't a dangerous place though at night it was eerie.

Mr. Kuput's Adventures

It was shortly after Elaine returned that I first met Mr. Kuput. It was at the museum while Elaine and I were looking at a new exhibit put in there for the Fall. Mr. Kuput was looking at the same things and he commented about a work of art to us as we passed him. He began talking (mostly about art) and he then asked us to join him for dinner as his guests. We looked at each other and then Elaine accepted for the both of us. So we joined Mr. Kuput—he never told us his first name that day— for dinner as his guests at a Middle Eastern restaurant across from the museum's main entrance. It was a nice evening, with Mr Kuput doing most of the talking at dinner, as Elaine was starved and so was I. He told us he had an apartment in the city fairly close to the museum and he also told us that he worked only three days per week—on Monday, Wednesday, and Friday. He seemed at first a bit gloomy but this aspect changed into a merriness that was infective for the most part though not put-offish at all and quite comical. We had fun with him that night and we exchanged phone numbers.

Mr. Kuput's adventures were many and varied. He never drove a car or took a bus if he didn't have to. He always went out on foot and walked wherever he was going, to the museum, to the park, or to the scene. He didn't make the scene very often but seemed to relish the fact that he could stay away from it for such long periods. When he did make it he never went to the college campus but only to the coffeehouse for coffee or hot cider and bread and cheese. He told me in confidence that he thought the scene to be a bit pathetic with all the freakish characters who loafed there. It was not that he disliked freaks but he seemed to have a nagging fear of them. It was this fear that kept him away from the coffeehouse for such long periods of time. It was probably why I never saw or noticed him at the scene even though he claimed to once have been a regular there. Perhaps that time was when I stayed away from the scene for a long period and didn't come back until about a year later. It was during a stretch of paranoia and depression that engulfed me for about a year and I hardly saw anyone during those days. But that was a long way away from the era with Elaine and now the new person, Mr.Kuput.

Mr. Kuput loved the museum. He went there quite often and would always be sure to go there for the special showings or events that came up from time to time. He dined at a lot of restaurants, especially the Middle-Eastern ones which he loved to eat in. He never ate lunch and rarely breakfast except when he was out and started the day early. He liked pizza late in the evening as a snack and he told me that he took speed once in a while to regulate his long sleeping habits. Also he said that speed helped him stay slim though in fact he had quite a stomach on him (probably from all the pizza).

Elaine grew to like him very much and the three of us began to see each other often. Several days a week we would meet either at his apartment or the museum cafeteria where he would prepare for a critical tour of his through the old or new exhibits. He was very critical of art and he thought himself to be a grand critic (which indeed he was, so articulately) and he would formulate artistic theories on the spur of the moment as we viewed a particular painting or sculpture. There was no limit to Mr. Kuput's knowledge. He was a master of art, literature, social science, and natural science. He knew advanced mathematics and even seemed t o have a sound knowledge of civil engineering and architecture. I thought perhaps that he had a doctorate in some field but I declined from asking him and he never mentioned college or degrees. This aspect of his character showed his humility as he never bragged about his own accomplishments, which must have been substantial. Elaine thought that he may have been a doctor but I disagreed with her on that point and we never discussed it again. We were too busy having adventures in our own world or, I should say, a world of our own making. There were no quick and easy trails to our lives. We just plodded onward and searched each day for an adventure which would fill our souls with inspiration and delight. We were never at a loss for things to do during the day or night and we continued to pursue our studies in all of this stimulating atmosphere which I must say Mr. Kuput helped bring about.

Elaine and I made a vow to stay together no matter what transpired between us or outside of us. We knew each other well enough to know when a certain adventure would be running out of steam and we knew when to be by ourselves and when to be with Mr. Kuput. We even spent a decent bit of time apart so that we could pursue other hobbies and other projects. Elaine had her poetry and I had my piano, though neither the poetry nor the piano really commanded as much attention those days as Mr. Kuput or the museum or dining at Middle Eastern restaurants. But with all that we did we were content and a peacefulness seemed to emerge gradually as the weeks passed that gave us a new perspective on the world we had made together. It was an ethereal time filled with adventures that went beyond the ordinary and yet had the peace and stillness of the rustic life. Yes, our pleasures were pastoral at times and we even still went once in a great while to the country to resume our studies of nature and wildflowers in the Fall, which is a great time for those things. We also went often to the park to roam over the place. I enjoyed Elaine's presence and Mr. Kuput made a great third party to our outings that Fall. October was on the cool side that year and all three of us loved every day of it. October is a special month for it is the true beginning of autumn and marks the time for a new era of adventures to begin. We began several new adventures in different parts of the city and we even once talked about a trip to New York to see operas and loaf in the Village. But we decided to wait for that for awhile mainly because we didn't want to leave Mr. Kuput and also because we were having such peaceful adventures in our own city that we hated to leave such a beautiful affair. We decided to stay home for Halloween and pass out candy to the children but we still would go out after it was over that night and perhaps meet Mr. Kuput for a snack and some coffee. I wanted very much to introduce Mr. Kuput to the college scene but I wasn't sure if he would want to go to a college campus. It was probably better that way after all.

Through the long nights before Elaine's return I wandered without meditation though with a calmness that could have been described as "peaceful" (as the peaceful adventures of the sixties were but they were different in that there was no central figure, such as Elaine was to me in those days, and there was more adventure than peace in the sixties, that was for sure) and contented with the knowledge that she was soon to come back to me in all her beauty and fiery spirit which characterized her jointly though separately as her beauty was definitely a thing in itself superimposed by her nature but secure in its evocation as a planet or even a star is secure in its orbit.

It was early September and I longed for Fall (October) and especially for the weather which would be fresh and cool unlike the heat of the past Summer which was most intense and undiminishing. I wondered much about whether or not Elaine would inspire me creatively when she returned as she had done so before her departure.

I also wondered whether I would ever master the study of music (which was my main endeavor back in those days) and I wished for a creative impulse before Elaine came back so that I would have a focus on which to work and something to develop in her presence. The thought of those past months without her made me sad but I saw in those passing months a new beginning for Elaine and me now that the hard part had been gone through. She would return with a burst of freedom and adventure like never before, I thought, as I lay down to go to sleep one night in early September when the speeding cars passed my window late at night and the screams of young men and women walking by outside my window made me think even more of her whom I missed so much that summer, the summer which was now coming to its end and thankfully I looked forward to a new and real autumn when everything would be different and I was secure in the fact of Elaine's return so much so that I even made plans for our first few days together, the first days also of Fall and I planned a trip to the museum for us to get reacquainted with each other for the length of our parting was substantial though I did not emphasize this aspect very much in my sleepy way of summoning up the events of the coming Fall as I used to do in the sixties for each new adventure begged for a preliminary description of itself. But those times were now lost forever amid a stream of memories which began with high school, especially the drinking parties and continued all the way up to and including the acid and speed days with Annie (which I mostly forgot now that Elaine was with me in an era so new and adventurous so as to stifle memories of old eras). The past no longer propelled me into fantasy and dreams of a new era that could be much like the past one. I was content and I contemplated things in so much an easier way than before Elaine came to me that I began to figure on a new life when she would return to the city she left so quickly almost six months before. There was nothing changed about the events I dreamed of that early September when the coolness already began to arrive and the trees were becoming yellow.

My piano practice was sluggish to say the least but I still pursued the piano with some vigor even though I didn't really like it as much as I used to. I just tried to get proficient at playing it and there were some good pieces to learn still so that I had an objective in mind during that time, that is to make it on the piano at all costs even if it meant losing Elaine. Perhaps Elaine's return would stymie that but I wasn't sure for the piano was central to my existence since I practiced every day without fail, especially Byrd's MY LADY NEVELL'S BOOKE OF VIRGINALL KEYBOARD MUSIC. I received great satisfaction from these pieces of Byrd and I continued to pursue them on the piano up until the time Elaine was to arrive in the city.

It was late September. She was to come in on a Saturday and I was prepared for her in all aspects of which I could be prepared for her return. I had several dreams about her in her absence and now these dreams would be coming true to some extent. I bought some new albums to play for her and I also bought her a book of poetry which she loved so much though I couldn't even understand why she loved it so.

She wrote quite a bit of poetry and once in awhile she would speed all night long and compose poems on the speed. This was a rare occasion for her though and she usually didn't speed though she smoked grass regularly even at parties where it was offered to her. She never drank except perhaps for some wine at a party and I liked this about her—that she never drank. While I waited for her to arrive I thought of her ass. It stuck out real nice and I was eager to see it naked and feel its crease. She had a nice crease.

Elaine and I spent some great days together that November and it was at Thanksgiving time that we went to a party at old Cd's farm again. It was an affair to remember with good food all over the place and great music.

The Desolate Land: Never leave the mountains.

One day in the mountains I took a strange road which led to a clearing and ended up in a dirt path just big enough for my Fiat. I rode down the path for several miles and took the turns so that, though I was not lost, I panicked several times at being lost in that valley and I would, I supposed, never find a way back to Elaine again. There was an abandoned car on the way back—and I looked in the front window and saw a bunny hanging by a cord from the rear view mirror. I wondered why someone had taken the bunny with him or her when they left the car there and it was strange and exciting to see that bunny hanging there. It was I know a childish pleasure but I loved looking at that thing even though I didn't take it as I easily could have because the front window of that car was open. For a week after that day I regretted not getting the bunny perhaps because it would be for Elaine, perhaps even for Mr. Kuput (who had a car but rarely drove it).

I went swimming late that afternoon and saw a girl with a cute rear who attracted my attention for several hours as I swam and sat by the side of the pool in the freshly cut grass on a large towel. I didn't talk to the girl though she once smiled at me as I stared her way. It could be a long time before I saw another like her but I said nothing and she left before I did without saying anything so I didn't feel all that badly though I realized that I had missed something at the pool that day.

As I returned one day from the hills I noticed that the city had become a desolate land. Bare trees, cold winds ravaged the buildings and streets and there was little trace of life there. I had forgotten to look for Elaine among the ruins of Schenley Park—the ruins that Summer left and had betrayed the park so shamelessly, that park where I had searched all Summer long for her, even into Indian Summer evenings when students from the nearby college that she used to attend would sit and stare into the early evening's sunset. Who could even imagine where she was? She was lost in a zone of time and place that gave no clues and emitted no words about her except that the memory of her presence lingered always at the old spots.

It seemed long ago that I knew her as if the world had brought her to her reward without so much as an advance invitation to any of her friends, old or new. She was a ghost of the ruined places, the old haunts where only memories abide. The Fall had arrived without her for the trees told of her departure in sounds that seemed to blast from the force of the winds of autumn. I wanted that October to forget about her, to rid my memory of her lovely face in the cool nights of October when festivals showed people having great times and farm parties emerged with no trace of her to dance and sing and ride the horses that were so dear to her. I thought about going to see Mr. Kuput but I kept putting the visit off as if even he would be pessimistic as to my chances for a renewal with her. A depression came over me; though not a deep one it still took hold of my body and spirit as never before and I began to see images of her face along the sides of large houses in the expensive districts of the city. I would imagine that she was living in a certain house and that she was so happy that she had forgotten all about me and the times we had with each other. I felt contented at those thoughts of her happiness for awhile but then the doubts started to plague me until I realized that I was just having the sweet dreams of depression. At times I wanted to cry in the night the names that I used to call her, hoping that one of those names would find a way to her ears and she would respond. Perhaps, I thought, I would find her one day in the Winter. But I remembered I thought the same thing the year before and it never happened. Sometimes I would think of Annie and even believe that the same thing was happening to Elaine, God forbid! The streets led to places I knew and cared for but I didn't stop anywhere as I drove on and on in my search.

There was no presidential election that November but I wanted there to be one so that I could forget what bothered me for so long. I resolved to see Mr. Kuput before Thanksgiving, perhaps even to spend that evening with him also if he would accept my invitation to dinner at an expensive place. In fact I looked forward to seeing him, remembering all his comforting days and nights in the long spell behind me. I didn't want to see Crazy Bob. His spurts of optimism didn't suit me then as they used to when we were better friends. Robert would be okay but he lived far away and I didn't want to call him because he always thought that my depression was never warranted but was an intellectual gimmick on my part, a mere front. Of course I would not bore Mr. Kuput with talk of past persons including that one person who so preoccupied my own mind. But just to be with him would compensate for a little time the weariness of depression and the lingering sadness that had come over me since the Summer ended. Not that Mr. Kuput was a substitute for the last one but he was always cheerful no matter what the situation or the setting. I would see him soon.

Victor E. Navarro, Jr.

The Desolate Land

I thought about the snow that was sure to come in late December and about other things which excited me though not as much as a deep snowfall. I applied for a job at the museum, and at the orientation there was a stupid film about bullshit's relationship to Andrew Carnegie. I thought I would never get out of there to meet Mr. Kuput at the museum café for some iced tea and cake but I finally got out of there to meet him at that cafe and we sat eating, drinking, and talking for over an hour and left to take a walk in the park. It was cool that day so I had on a sweater as did he and we talked on the walk about literature as usual with no mention of the lost girl, not even a hint of her. We had dinner at Ali Baba's where Mr. Kuput treated—we took turns taking checks at restaurants. He invited me back to his place but I told him I would meet him here after dark, as I wanted to check out a girl I recently saw for the first time in ten years. I went to her apartment and I explored sexual topics with her, overtly and verbally, and I left feeling eager to see Mr. Kuput and talk to him about contemporary literature, especially the novel.

We discussed the novel for several hours over coffee and pastries and then I went home not thinking whether to take speed because I wanted to stay up all night. I wanted to write a long letter to Elaine even though I didn't know where she was living. Speed would help me, I thought, so I took three tablets and began my trip at exactly midnight, starting to write the letter at about one o'clock in the morning. The letter came slowly but succinctly and after a while I was pleased with it and I planned to proceed the rest of the night writing that letter that she would probably never read. But I had thought that some day I would show it to her even though it was written on Ritalin and she would not approve of that.

The long trips to the hills continued and I searched for Elaine's face in the crowds of hills. I thought one day that her face could be carved in a tree trunk waiting for me to set upon it. I was filled with wonder about her, especially her disappearance, and I surmised that she was lost in some valley, possibly the next one as I drove on, and she would only be found in Winter. Such thoughts came to me on those sun-filled drives into the hills and I even started to hallucinate little Elaine scampering about the grassy hills of one or another ski resort. I made a vow to myself to do some skiing the coming Winter unlike the Winters before when I put it off because of the long drive. The last time I skied was with Dorrie years before and I had a great time sliding down the slopes and trails and riding the chairlift. In fact one day that Summer I took the longest chairlift to the summit just as a lark and thought of her while I rode upward towards the peak. She was not at the top as I had imagined on my way up but I still looked around for her and became frustrated at the futility of my search. She would not, after all, be found in the mountains. I imagined I would find Elaine in the city on a Summer evening just as I once found Annie in the park in June of the year she went away. Mr. Kuput and I could look for her at Flagstaff Hill and the surrounding park and maybe we would find her there with a new boyfriend—I dreaded the thought—or with a girlfriend just sitting on the hill waiting for the movie to start. There was a movie twice a week so that would be a good start. I would love to tell Mr. Kuput to join me in the park for the movie in the night when everything is so much quieter than in the day. Of course the mountains were quiet in the day, almost an eerie stillness that never lessened even with the roar of a passing car engine. It was late August when Mr. Kuput and I went to the film one night at Flagstaff Hill. Summer was coming to an end as we both could tell from the mild chill of the evening. I told him that I would continue my daily trips to the hills into the Fall and he suggested that I do even more than that. He told me to go further into the ranges so that I could think out my position as regarded Elaine whom he missed almost as much as I and to whom he once told that she was lucky to have me. This he told me the night of the movie and I was glad that he did as we both liked the movie and discussed it afterward at his apartment over coffee. He was a real big coffee drinker and he even had it late at night though I had just one cup that night. I went home thinking about what I would do the next evening after my daily trip and I resolved to see Mr. Kuput again because he advised me so well.

 The long rolls of the road in front of me, as I drove faster and faster, dipped and bent in the valleys and hills and gave me a feeling of peace I had not experienced in some time. There were motels along the way and country inns like I had never seen and I stopped at some of them, especially the inns, to get a drink and a sandwich. I ate all of my dinners at Seven Springs where they had a buffet every night. I ate late dinners beginning in early September. I thought about taking Crazy Bob with me on an outing because he always said he wanted to visit the mountains. But he would break the chain of days I had spent there and I didn't want to do that because of the peace I had acquired there and he was too talkative for a trip to the mountains. I longed for October when the leaves would change colors and fall all over the fields and valleys where I would stop the car and walk for some time remembering Elaine and the autumn walks with her. If I could only find her, I thought, and take her up to the ranges with me we would have such a time. We could make the rounds and end up at Seven Springs for dinner, perhaps even get a room there and stay overnight. I wished I could share all of that with her but I realized that it wouldn't be for some time until I found her and I gave up the intense search in the city after I had returned from my days in the mountains. I was seeing Mr. Kuput almost every night though he was not very interested in seeing me during the day. I couldn't understand why but I still didn't ask him and I forgot about it when he said that he liked to sleep until 3PM. I left in the early mornings for the hills and that would exclude him. We did meet at night though and he was very pleasant to me and helped me slip out of my depressions just as quickly as I slipped into them. My depressions were caused by Elaine's absence—I knew that to be the cause of them—but I still was feeling depressed even when she was with me before. Perhaps it was the speed, I told myself. I wanted to tell Elaine that I thought so much about her during the trips to the mountains and I wanted to tell her more than that too. My little yellow Fiat rode well on the country roads and took the sharp turns at pretty good speed—the steering was great. I couldn't predict where I would be in a few months but I knew that the mountains would be large on the horizon of my dreams.

THE DESOLATE LAND

At the onset of the trip of the Fiat—a search for the First Deity, perhaps God, perhaps not—I took several drives to the mountains where I would get lost on the back roads and in the deep valleys so near to where I was headed yet so far from the real road I wanted to travel that I would panic in my yellow Fiat as if the end came unexpectedly and I was unprepared for it. It was in the Summer of the First, those drives, and I wondered the whole time what would come of them just as I surmised that I was fortunate to have a car to search the hills for the First. On those trips I thought often of Elaine. Perhaps, I thought one sunny afternoon while driving through a serene valley, Elaine would be found in the mountains. It was as if a dream suddenly occurred on a trip through a verdant scene which gave little background for the dream but still encouraged it, since I couldn't forget about her, I traveled toward her. The trips to the mountains became a regular thing and there were days when I stopped for a swim or went to the resort tucked deep into the range of hills that were so familiar to me in August. Getting lost in those hills was rare but such a strange thrill that I looked forward to it, just as I searched the countryside for traces of Elaine in my memories of the old days, days that I hoped would arrive soon again, though they only surfaced in my memory filtered by the sudden changes in landscape and terrain. In the mountains I experienced many new adventures that gave way to sudden bouts of despair which were natural from the loss I suffered. But the trip of the First spurred me onward further into the spell of hills and valleys.

I would stop at suburban malls and browse at books for hours before and after treks to the deep ranges.

So Elaine was on my mind totally through the daily trips to the mountains and I didn't want to forget about her. I also looked for her in the evenings when I returned from the day's outings to Flagstaff Hill where they had concerts and movies almost every night. One night I saw her friends there but not her, but I didn't talk to them because I didn't like them very well when she was in college. That night was the only time I saw a trace of Elaine through that long Summer of torment and fascination for the hills and valleys I traversed by car every day. I would stop at malls each day and buy things like sleazy underwear to turn on a girl I might meet at the swimming pool or at one of the mountain resorts I frequented almost every day. The underwear came in different colors and fit extremely tight. My ass looked pretty good through the women's panties. They came three in a carton and I brought many cartons of them on my trips to and from the hills. I thought also of Mr. Kuput though I didn't see him often any more because I wanted to pursue the girls for sex and he was far too old to join me. I thought of going to a massage parlor but that was not what I wanted. I wanted the real thing, simply and purely. Massage parlors were a last resort. I saw many pretty girls in the mountains, especially at Seven Springs resort where one waitress I had was so sexy that I tried for her but she had a date that night. Perhaps another time I thought and watched her sun bathe in a bikini in between shifts.

I rode the chairlift towards the summit and thought how great it would be to have Elaine with me. I had never taken Elaine skiing though I wanted to. She was shy of going but I should have forced her, I thought, as I headed to the top of one of the slopes of Seven Springs Mountain. After reaching the top, I walked the entire long way down the mountain and took the lift back up and again wished Elaine could be with me and become as exhilarated as I was then.

Though the trip of the First was not my prime consideration I was still into it heavily. The beginning of madness did not deter me from exploring the First in such detail but I often neglected my search for Elaine to pursue the First.

It would be two years ago that upcoming Thanksgiving that Elaine and I dined with Mr. Kuput. The three of us would not be together this time and I didn't look forward to that evening very much even though I probably could spend it with one of the other two people I liked so much. But this was only early October and there was still a chance, I thought, that she would return in time for at least one of the three seasonal holidays of my liking: Halloween, Thanksgiving, and Christmas. It would be nicest if she would return for Christmas so that I could lavish on her the gifts I had saved for her during the two years she had gone. But more important than the gifts I would have her back with me to spend the long winter in the city and also in the mountains and Mr. Kuput could join us often in our days and nights together in the snow-filled world of that most beautiful of seasons. Perhaps even we would have a friend for him for he talked often of dating someone (probably for pleasure, but I really didn't know what for exactly).

The days were getting shorter and shorter and the winds were chilled a bit off and on so as to give a transitional effect from the past Summer. The true Fall was almost here as the trees showed their colors almost fully. Leaves covered the sidewalks around my house and especially the park where they filled the paths with yellow and brown and made all seem enmeshed in a golden hue. Gold as the color of the expensive ring I once gave her. Mr. Kuput adored it. He once told me that it was the perfect gift. I was very pleased to hear this from him and I thought about getting a bracelet to match it. But that was some time ago and now there was no ring nor its wearer. Both had vanished into the past Winters and a new Winter now approached, slowly winding through the sun's positions in the sky as if nothing could ever change in the aspects of those positions, when suddenly one notices that it is dark before six o'clock and cooler than in April and soon it will be Halloween. I asked Mr. Kuput if he handed out candy on that evening and he said he did just as I did every evening of that special day. Like a child, I looked forward to it and when it came I cherished each moment of it.

MR. KUPUT

Mr. Kuput emerged like an old friend from childhood that I had not seen in a long time in a ruined city park where Elaine and I used to walk. He came in those times when just about all seemed to last forever amid the trees of a cool October. The last thing I would have guessed about him was that he was wealthy. He dressed well but he didn't have the air of a wealthy man even though he loved to pay for the coffees at the museum. When a day would pass without seeing him I would miss his presence and think of how nice it would be when I could once again be with him. He became almost a full replacement for Elaine.

I still continued my trips to the mountains into October and the colors of those hills were exciting to see, especially around the resort. I took walks up and down the ski trails that I used to ski as a teenager in the sixties. I would even cut class to go skiing then and I resolved on one walk to ski during the upcoming Winter at least once, perhaps more. I considered the adventures of skiing and I decided to ask Mr. Kuput to join me for a day at the resort in Winter even though he probably couldn't ski—he could sit in the lodge while I was outside and we could be together the rest of the time for I took short runs when I skied. Elaine used to come with me to ski. I wanted to recapture just this with Mr. Kuput not as if he had totally replaced Elaine but as an adventure that evokes past fulfillments. He once mentioned that he was a lover of mountains in Winter. I would ask him soon.

I drove all over the place in those days as if there were nothing else but my car to sustain me besides Mr. Kuput. Of course he was more to me than cruising and I didn't drive much at night as I would be with him after my daily trips.

Forgotten journeys are always adventurous when they occur but they leave nothing for the mind.

Each day I thought about Elaine, sometimes constantly, often enough to inspire me to be at my next meeting with Mr. Kuput. There were few adventures that October and in the space of about two weeks I didn't even go to any resorts or on any trips because they began to depress me—I would hear conversations in the restaurants that were inane to me. I looked forward during the days to my meetings with Mr. Kupt in the evenings. I would talk to him without depression even though I may have had a depressing day. He always cheered me up and he gave me courage to face the next day as if I had had a burst of Ritalin during our evening meetings. I was not taking speed though I craved it sporadically. Of course I had a large supply of it that I kept just in case I changed my mind.

The searches of those days never seemed to end. October was always a long month though one of my favorite distractions was dining with Mr. Kuput, which made the time pass more easily. After dining he would either go to his apartment or to my house, but mostly it was his place at his own request. Once in awhile we would stop at the college campus and have cokes and talk for some time about the people who were attending school then. I was always startled at how much they had changed in college from when Elaine first went there. I could barely believe that it was the same place I used to frequent: it had changed so much as the new students were so different from the old ones I had known. They were pale like ghosts and the number of nerds seemed to have increased geometrically each year so that most of the students were now nerds—the opposite of what I had known years before. A nerd is easy to spot on sight and the error factor is minimal. That campus produced nerds by the thousands and it was almost very depressing except that I was in the company of Mr.Kupt who gave a humorous reflection to it all. Nerds were to be laughed at, I learned, and they soon no longer depressed me. A nerd may contribute much to society but a nerd is a pathetic figure sometimes. Until Mr. Kuput showed me the funny side of nerds I despised them, but after he showed me their hapless situations I saw that they were harmless creatures who really didn't bother anyone and who just seemed to vegetate back and forth from one computer room to another. They ate sparingly at the snack bar and usually drank milk. They also consumed much fruit. Mr. Kuput said that they were like human clones in a world of white clones. They somehow lost their purity and became nerds. Though nerd-baiting had been a sport I once liked it no longer was with Mr. Kuput. Still I felt no love for those creatures. Anyway they never smoked cigarettes or even pipes.

The walks that I used to take with Elaine were important to me. The changing of the seasons along with her presence made that Fall the most delightful of times. We both thought of Mr. Kuput and of how long it was since we saw him. He was such a great person that we felt it a bit of a shame that we hadn't contacted him sooner or later. But that notion passed and we resumed our daily routine of walks in the afternoon and creative sessions at night. We would try each day to walk a little bit more until we reached a goal of several hours, which was not all that much considering we did nothing in the afternoon anyway. Crazy Bob rarely joined us on the walks though he did participate in one day's walking which turned out to be unusual. The three of us were headed down a path in Frick Park, a path which we were not used to traveling, and we suddenly came upon a dead dog just near the border of the path. Elaine went up to the dog and almost shrieked at the gruesome sight which confronted her. Crazy Bob wanted to bury the dog in a deeper part of the woods under leaves but we decided against it for it would not be safe to lift the decaying carcass and to carry it anywhere. We were all three of us shaken up from that experience and Elaine and I never went down that particular path again.

Winter was headed our way as November rolled in quickly and the ground became colorful and dead to a life of summertime just a few months before. When that month came I began to think of the silent dignity and its problems and I became for a time depressed over the state of things though I never was deeply depressed. It was a depression I could live with and I gradually worked my way out of it but it took some time, and I was still feeling the effects of my discoveries of Thanksgiving when we went to Mr. Kuput's apartment for a festive dinner. Mr. Kuput appeared to be wealthy though I had some doubts about that appearance. Elaine thought he was very rich and we disagreed about him on that point as we did on other points as well. Elaine thought him to be self-educated while I thought him formally educated to a high degree, perhaps with a doctorate, in some field. We argued about this for several days until we agreed to drop the subject because it was coming between us so much in those days.

Mr. Kuput became my consoler in those times and he was very good at it. The role occupied him quite a bit and he told me that I was welcome any time at his apartment. We took some trips to the museum together and he criticized the art less, giving me a chance to deal with my personal crisis, and at the same time being less obtrusive than usual, he spoke rarely as I knew that he knew the shape I was in. The company of that man made life more bearable for me and I thanked him for his ministrations over dinner one night. It was better having him around than it would have been to have Crazy Bob following me about during that era. I did not see Crazy Bob that

Spring and since he didn't like Elaine all that much it was best for me not to see him until the whole thing passed over if it ever would.

One night in April I went to Mr. Kuput's place as a depression engulfed my mind so deeply that I didn't walk that day but just sat in my sofa in the living room thinking about my current state of affairs and mind.

Mr. Kuput was glad to see me though it was after nine and he fixed me a glass of iced tea and some cookies that he had bought that same day. We talked about literature that night, especially about a new novel that had just come out late that Winter by a Pittsburgh writer in his early twenties. Mr. Kuput told me stories that night that helped my depression and he seemed quite concerned with my mental state just as he was worried about Elaine and her onset of delusions. He told me he hadn't seen her lately but that she was on his mind often. I didn't want to talk about her so I changed the subject to world history and that occupied us the rest of the night until midnight, when I left the apartment and drove back home, feeling more alert and less down than during the day.

The past rolled forth from my memory like a tidal wave rolls onto the coast. For years I cherished certain eras of the past and it was these same eras that sprang forth to meet the present with Elaine. I recalled Annie and her struggles to keep sane along with George H.'s drug dealings and Arthur's hallucinations of greatness. In Arthur's case, I attributed the state of origin to an egotism that never faded, a self-love that was at times all-embracing. Whatever became of those three persons from past eras I didn't know but I was sure they were still living in a world filled with sorrow and dreams of creative passion that even years afterwards lingered in my own heart. Nothing would ever be said about them, lost as they were for good, that would include a description of their <u>mals</u>, except perhaps to say it was the madness of the times that drove them insane. I didn't know and I didn't want to know. I was content with their selves wrapped neatly within my brain for some cold day in December when all else was failing me. Elaine knew that I had those memories and she begged me not to give them up for anything, even her. I thought that perhaps she would never replace those lost days in my dreams but I also thought that I could be mistaken about those times just as I once thought her too good for me.

On one of the walks I remembered Karen, and how she so much wanted to have a friend. Perhaps it was a true friend she wanted for she had many friends but possibly they were false friends and not up to her expectations. Karen was the kind of person that was snippy at first but very nice once you got to know her. She occupied a special place in my memories along with Ellen and some others though I suppose that Ellen and Karen were the most prominent members of my nostalgic vocabulary. Ellen was long gone from when I knew her. She kept up our friendship from far away for awhile but eventually it dwindled into just a memory as things usually work out when friends move far away for good. Karen was the same and I never heard from her after the sixties although I did hear from her sister about her and her new family —she had three children and was doing well and I was glad to hear that. I saw her sister at a restaurant one night about eight years after I last saw Karen. Hearing about her sparked a rush of memories that kept me going for about a month and even longer in which I was involved in a gallant return to a lost era, an era that wouldn't go away and kept pushing its way forward into the future as if it refused to be lost in time.

Elaine was a good replacement for Karen and because of that fact I became closer to Elaine as well as for other reasons like the things we had in common, her looks, and her pleasant nature. Her looks were better than Karen's and she gave me what I wanted as opposed to what I needed. That was an important factor in our bonding, and I would tread endlessly on it because it was so wonderful to me to have her so childishly vulnerable yet so passionate in her basic nature. She was more intense than Annie was and she had more going for her than Karen and Annie put together. All of these things contributed to my ardent desire for Elaine and made me more and more conscious that she was finally the right person for me.

I was more critical of people at that point than I was in the sixties and more discriminating of whom I associated with. I lacked some of the vigor of those earlier days yet I still had energy and desire to go with my new sensibilities and outlook. At times I still wished Ellen to be around to be my friend and confidant in happy as well as troubled times. But I realized that this could never be and I was resolved to quit thinking of Ellen so much that November just before the drive on that big day with Mr. Kuput.

I took walks in the evening starting in mid-November alone and I began to feel less encumbered about my being with Elaine and at the same time more free and easy in my dealings with the world. The world never changes when we are content and that was the way I wanted it to be all winter at least as I started out that season with expectations of a glorious time for me and Elaine and less time given to the past with more to be spent on our friendship, which began to flower so positively and beautifully. Though the past I knew would never go away, I hoped to recapture it only when I needed to do so, not unannounced as usual but at my command for my own personal enjoyment and for literary reasons.

As the Winter began, with its cold weather, I started to see things differently as I did every change of season but more pointedly in the coming of Winter, my favorite time of the year. With the holidays coming I decided to make them a special event in my life if not forever then for this year at least. This would be difficult for we are so addicted to the ordinary course of events that we forget how to make special times of special ones. But I decided to at least try to make this holiday season the best of what preceded it and I vowed to try to make Elaine as happy as I ever saw her. She never wore a sad face as long as I knew her, but I wanted her happiness to increase, to overflow. The joys of that future Christmas were in front of me as I walked the evenings away thinking of how to please her the most, the best way, in the upcoming festivities of the arriving season.

While I was searching what to find in the way of literature to read and digest I found an old math book. Math started getting to my brain as I read the book. Functions interested me quite a lot as well as other topics. But my main penchant was still for literature—the right literature. I must say I enjoyed Elaine's writing though she wrote mostly poetry. I tried to get her to write longer fiction but she stuck for the most part to poetry. That was one of the things I didn't like about her. The other things were less trivial like the fact that she always talked about herself, her own accomplishments, her own thing. This amazed me somewhat but she did it in such an endearing manner that I overlooked the expressiveness of her writing and focused my attention on her style.

She was about as unlike Annie as night is from day. Annie was a more sincere person who tried to please. Elaine could care less whether she pleased. The difference between them was enormous. One night in mid-July I decided to write to Elaine, hoping that she would respond in some fashion either by letter or by phone, if not in person, about her returning to me as soon as possible. (Robert would have gone and dragged her back bodily but I found methods that obtained her interest.) She responded other times, but why not this time? As I wrote her I thought of Barbara and how she hated Elaine. It was back in Elaine's and Barbara's college days—they both attended the same college at the same time—and knew one another:

Barbara always had a comment about Elaine, even at times referring to her as the "blond ditz." Barbara once told me she thought Elaine to be very gross but she was indeed prejudiced about Elaine as I liked them both at the same time though I must say I liked Elaine more and that made Barbara angry even to the point of being furious. I felt sad about Barbara's fate in our trio but she may have deserved it for she was so selfish that many people thought her to be a creep, including the Dude, who told me to avoid her. I used to call her "Dah" and she would not even respond to that nicety as I lavished kisses to her forehead even though she was mad at me about something stupid like the way she said I was treating her. It's funny but I treated her well, I thought, taking her to dinner every night at the finest restaurants. But she still thought I was not treating her well, and that cemented itself into her stubborn mind like an axe in a tree. But that was long ago and it was over with long ago and I didn't care anymore except that I felt a little sad when I thought of Barbara and the warranted suspicions about me and Elaine. A walk in the snow had cured me of Barbara but that did not respite when Elaine came to my mind. Elaine was a product of my blood, a by-product which flows towards the heart and keeps it alive and fresh for each new day. But I thought of the day when we would no longer be together and that was probably inevitable even though it had already, in a way, come. Fortune seemed to be dispelled by a growing feeling of distrust between us, a distrust which began to consume both of us even though she was the one to blame in all infidelity and transgression. Literature would calm my soul. Perhaps I should return to Hemingway? I pondered over these things but I didn't arrive at any conclusion. Elaine would probably have to return before I felt better about things, including literature (of which she was a master in her own right). I thought of reading some of her poetry to remember her by but I couldn't bring myself to do it, no matter how low I felt. I couldn't do it.

July passed and with it the unbearable heat that enveloped the city. Elaine did not answer my letter of the end of the first week in August. I was angry.

Victorious Illusions

Walks in the park were good for me and I knew it. I took many of them that summer and I started to acquire a longing for Fall on one of the walks in early August. Fall was a good time for me as I liked the death and eventual renewal (Spring) of nature. The longing for Fall usually begins in August and lasts into October until the true autumn weather emerges from the northeast. The park combined many elements of mystery and fun for me as it did in my younger days when things were bathed in sunlight as far as my memory goes. In the park that Summer I walked on and on several miles each day and I must admit I thought of Elaine quite often during those walks. But even more than her I thought of nature—the stars and galaxies of the night and how they would appear after the sun went down. I walked in the evening and after dark—twice each day—one time for exercise, the other time for contemplation. Things came to me on those walks such as the total number of stars in the universe that I was later to think could be found on some rock deep in the woods at the countryside where I used to hike. There were no more trips to the Open Pantry that summer, I was too lazy to walk there and, as I did my walking at night, I didn't want to be out after dark in those neighborhoods. Anyway the Open Pantry was a far trip and it was in fact too far to handle that summer.

I got lazy because of Elaine and I decided not to venture too far from home as I would venture far with her in the Summer by car. I never permitted her to drive because she was so reckless and careless at the wheel.

When I first met her she wrecked my new Fiat coupe and ever since then I was wary of her driving. But that was long before the Summer of her absence. In between there were the farm parties with the wild dancing and the parties at Arthur's in the city where there were drugs galore. I could see them all, all those parties on Brighton Avenue back in the old days (though in fact those days were not so old as they appeared to be). I thought on my walks in the park of Annie and Arthur and how they almost got married to each other years ago when everything was more calm, more peaceful. The adventures of the days of long past were so peaceful that you looked forward to them each night—like at Ellen's apartment in 1967 when the Fall was so fresh to the lungs and Mildred and I played football and darts together to pass the early evening.

Victorious Delusions
A Tale of the Late 1960's

A long time before I met Elaine there was a peaceful adventure every night. This was back in the sixties when things were more adventurous than ever before or ever after. The times were great in that there were things you could do that were exciting as things always are in the late teens and early twenties. Drugs were a big part of the sixties but they dwindled in use and effect into the early seventies so that there was little drug-taking for a time that still had the peaceful adventures that were so prevalent in the sixties.

Elaine was just a little girl in the late sixties while I was heavily into speed and acid and I couldn't stop those addictions for love or money. Money was prevalent at the time and I had no trouble paying for drugs even though they were, for the most part, cheap at that time. I would chronicle those adventures but it wouldn't be to anyone's advantage except my own and thus I will not do so. But I must say that those adventures live on only in my memory and probably in the memories of those others who lived them along with me back in the sixties. Annie, especially, was one of those people. Elaine was not. Thus there was a gap between me and Elaine, a gulf which could never be bridged because of the distance between our ages. But Elaine was a drug user of the hugest proportions. She liked speed and Quaaludes and also smoked grass and dropped acid quite often. She even took cough syrup when there was nothing else available and she drank on occasion. I never drank and I didn't like to see her ever drink but she did it all the same at parties which in those days were events so it was not too bad; the drinking she did, that is. Annie never

never drank but was a big drug user, especially on speed as she always was. Arthur and Annie later started speeding heavily together at about the time I got my first large supply of the stuff. But that was another era in itself, separated from Elaine's era as it was another universe. Gone were the days of speed and grass on the condom as well as kinky sex. Ron Dondril's wine on the condom became a big thing with his fellow speed freaks as was initiated wine-drinking on speed condoms for the whole scene of speed freaks whom he came to know and admire as well as lay often with. But then again Ron Dondril was a thing of the past never to be seem again after he freaked out and wound up in a state hospital all drugged out on speed and acid.

Many adventures I had with Annie back in the old days –and I had them also with Arthur who eventually drifted away from the scene and went South to live. Those days were filled with a peacefulness which I had not yet attained with Elaine. Elaine inspired more turbulent times and less peaceful adventures. A peaceful adventure is an adventure which one can look back on with tranquility and see the actual peace that was achieved by it. In the sixties there were many such peaceful adventures and I remember most of them except for some of the times I had with Karen and Ellen in the Fall of 1967. I remember those less perhaps because of the frequency of them and the fact that Karen and Ellen occupied so much of my time and life back in those days. Forgotten also were the times I had in the Summer of that year when I was straight for awhile and not into drugs as much as I was in the winter, spring and fall of that year. The Summer had one big adventure though and that was at Ocean City, New Jersey. I stayed for two weeks and I loved the whole time I spent there. I had speed only once the time I was there and spent a good deal of time walking on the shore down to the bay and back to the city.

There were plenty of girls I met while there and I did enjoy their company as I wandered to and from the main area of shops and cafes from which I wouldn't report until late each night. Robert worked down there for the summer and I saw him often when he was not working. Of course he drank and I didn't so that separated us infinitely. But I still saw enough of him to enjoy his presence. Alan M. was also down there at the time and he joined Robert and me on our adventures. I got a grand tan in the wind and sun and my hair turned slightly blond through it all. Wanderings along the beach were my favorite times in Ocean City and when I left I was very healthy from all of that exposure to the ocean air and sun. My aunt had a house in the Gardens and I stayed there most of the two weeks. I had formerly spent an entire summer at her house two years before after I graduated from high school. The beauty of the place left me feeling good and I returned home to the city in grand spirits. Fresh and clean was my body and soul from exposure to the ocean climate and I was ready for the Fall term at the university to study mathematics and philosophy which were my two majors in college. I was ready.

This was before I knew Karen and Ellen and it would be a while before they came into my life though I had several girlfriends in the meantime which didn't last all that long. I spent a lot of time with Jim and he discussed Zen and the hippies. Jim said that Zen was a part of the Journey to the East but I disagreed. I told him one night over the phone that Zen had nothing to do with the Journey. He got mad at me for this statement but he forgot about it and remained friends with me. The Journey to the East had intrigued me since I read the novel by that title by Hesse and I thought of myself on such a Journey, a Journey not to end very quickly. It was a long journey, not a mere sojourn, though some sojourns last a long time like the one in Marjorie Rowling's THE SOJOURNER. It is a strange book but a great one by my standards, even though it is a bit depressing. But I didn't mind sad books in those days so I read them, especially at night (though rarely while on speed).

When on speed I mostly wrote and listened to music (especially classical music) and once in awhile stayed out all night and had rapping sessions with fellow speed freaks. That Summer I didn't miss speed at all and I recovered from all the speed I took before the summer during what was the speed era of eras.

I could not put down NAZRITE LORDS that Summer and I was heavily into Zen and read a dozen books about that subject during June, July and August. I read mostly on my grandmother's porch during the day. I went out with Jim at night but I didn't drink at all and took speed rarely as I was never to return to the speed days again.

At least I was never to return to such intense speeding, although I was to increase my time drinking and acid tripping substantially.

There was a trip in late August with the inimitable George H. to Boston and a speed orgy of unreal proportions which I had not had since the Spring with Annie and Arthur. But loafing with George H. always led to bizarre antics, such as tripping on acid or speed or both. I avoided him after the trip until through him I met Allen and then he faded from the scene as he moved to the District of Columbia (D.C.). He no longer terrorized the scene with his brash ways and it wasn't a bad way to leave the scene as he sold some acid real cheap to get rid of it because he was leaving for D.C.

All of my illusive victories from Annie's decline to the Trip of the First (and others) were shrouded in a mystery of adventure that I didn't find in the days with Elaine. Things weren't the same with her. There were of course adventures but not of the same force by which the old adventures made their mark. Things went less smoothly with Elaine and sometimes I thought that perhaps I was being fooled by her like a false sense of creativity –something I never doubted in the lost days with Annie and something that I used to never doubt within myself in those old times of peaceful adventures. But in the new era I found a way to make things—every day things—beautiful in their own right. I found a sensual outlet for my addictive urges and I also found glimpses of the old peace that encompassed everything in the lost times of Annie and Arthur. Gone was the speeding that I used to do so much of. Gone also was the literature of the era—there was little or no literature in Elaine's era but an urge to experience like never before. Experience was the key in those days and I explored so many uncounted things that I never ceased to be enticed by one experience or another. Perhaps it was Elaine's presence which cast the spell needed to engender in one the desire for varied experiences. It was a dormant urge, and it never seemed to emerge during my times with Annie.

Long gone were the days of romance and adventure that were the late sixties. They were followed by less exciting and slower-paced times—the seventies—and a more stable flow of days and events and experiences which comprised the new era. Elaine became an important part of that era. In fact she was the focal point from which emerged the various experiences and subtle adventures which gave me a feeling of being alive similar to that feeling the sixties gave me but different in many respects. The sixties was a time of great change while the new era was a time of stability. A new awareness emerged from the ashes of the old era and encompassed everything from love-life to artistic pursuits and there was also a way of seeing things that was different from my old way. For instance the way I viewed art at the museums was quite different. In the old days art was for me a passion, an ever-present flowing of feeling and ideas which never ceased. In the new era art became a more tranquil past-time of a long and arduous search for beauty in nature and in created forms. The search had some difficult times to it but it was self-contained and gave one the feeling of experiencing truth to its highest points.

However the spirit of art seemed to be lost in the past just as Annie was lost in her illusions that never went away and made her an invalid.

Elaine had no illusions or delusions about anything. She was open-minded and gave her best to her writing which became over a period of time quite fluent. She rarely indulged in self-criticism though she was critical of art and of others. Her approach to art was one of detachment and she never abandoned herself to passion even when creating forms in her writing which gave the evidence of a long thought-out process in which there were many ways of seeing what she was doing by writing the way she did. So often she would want to be left alone so she could write; and this much I granted her, knowing that she loved to create by her writing.

Compared to Annie's painting and writing, Elaine's writing was filled with realistic details all of which reflected her desire to remake reality to fit some other form of reality. She preferred contemporary art to ancient art and she saw no need to read Homer or any other classics. I tried unsuccessfully to get her into George Eliot as a study for the novel she wanted to write but she would have nothing to do with that author for reasons which were not really clear to me. She didn't like parody or biography and she hated Shakespeare though she admitted his greatness. Just as Annie painted abstract portraits of those she knew in the late sixties, I began to compose a portrait of Elaine in my writings. I began in the middle of October and by early November I had compiled several pages of writing about Elaine. I felt it was good and that she would be pleased with it. Being a writer she would know what if anything was lacking in my compositions (which included poetry as well as prose) and she would be able to judge as to what should be done with it—should it be committed to the flames (as Hume said), or should it be kept for our own sakes and for memory's sake.

The long October was ended with a not so populated Halloween night when she and I gave out candy at my house until after nine and then we went for dinner at a small restaurant which was not busy at all for a Saturday night. We hoped we would run into Mr. Kuput for we didn't want to call on him until that Thanksgiving when we were invited to his beautiful condominium. We were both looking forward to that event, and we bought him a contemporary book that we thought he would enjoy reading, as he told us he liked such books. We also stuck some of Elaine's poems, neatly typed, into that book, because on another occasion he had read and admired immensely some of her poems. They were not romantic poems, of course, but were verses of nature with allusions to ancient times and mixed in with anecdotes from her early adventures when she was in high school. She told me she took acid once while at boarding school and sat in a closet for most of the trip. She freaked out quite badly, I assumed, from the way she told it to me. Her story lacked animation, though, and I wondered whether she was telling me the truth and not just bragging that she took acid in high school. In fact she was fond of acid and took it often when I first knew her in college, but lately she didn't take it much. Speed was her bag now and she relished the times I could get it for her. She claimed that it helped her write better. In fact she said that the only time she ever wrote was while she was speeding. The day before Halloween I gave her three Ritalin tablets and she put them in a safe place for future use. I didn't want her to abuse the stuff but I did supply her with it when I got some of it.

November is a strange month because it is a transition from one season to the next. All during the early days of that month I searched for a meaning to Elaine's madness but found none. She was becoming more and more elusive to me each day and I was alarmed at the prospect of her fading away from me. Just as Annie faded away from me during our last days, Elaine had the same symptoms though not as acute as Annie's were. I remembered a comment Arthur made to me years ago that still echoed in my thoughts like the knell of a black day yet to come. He told me that one day I would drive a woman insane with my style. I wasn't too concerned about it at the time but with Elaine on a walk one day I remembered exactly what he had said and how he had said it, but I dismissed it all as paranoia and continued to treat Elaine in the same manner, catering to her childlike whims and fancies and just plainly being nice to her. After all she was my lady since I had no real lady to take care of and since she was so vulnerable that it was hard not to care for her as a child lost in a harsh city and unaware of the dangers that lurked everywhere for such a child. Her prettiness too made it even more obvious to me that she was vulnerable, at least to prospective rapists who looked for prettiness to violate. But this mesh of things concerning her led me almost to the point of madness but I abandoned treating her like a baby after a while though I still viewed her as one. There was nothing in her life which compelled her to do anything. Her family was very wealthy and she had lots of free time to spend thinking about whatever she wished. She went to the museum often and on walks with me every day and she appeared quite happy and even more sane than I could hope for. She hadn't changed since when I first knew her while she was in college and there was a long time in between then and the days of her affections for me. Though some days are lost in the alleys of time, other days remain in the forefront, always in the picture. It is from those days that we take our communion of memories to the present and future and never let down on our histories as if they were always there in front of us begging for attention like a starving dog of the streets. What we lose from the past we also gain as much or more from it because of its vastness like mountains of snow.

All during the nights of that November I searched for a way to surprise Elaine, perhaps with something unusual that could make her excited—she got excited so infrequently that she irked me because of this and at times I thought her to be bored with me, though when I confronted her about it she said that she wasn't bored at all. It was funny but Crazy Bob thought her to be boring. He once told me so while she was in a ladies room but he told me never to repeat it to her because he liked her very much and he said if she and I were not together he would pursue her frantically. He had known her since her college days also. In fact it was he who introduced me to her for the first time in the small bar of the college just as it was he who first told me she liked me. But his place in our relationship soon faded due to other circumstances than his style and she stopped seeing him completely when she left school. But that Fall he returned with a loud bang into our lives and he was exactly the same as when we first knew him years before.

And so Elaine was keeping herself in some other city far away from me. It was indeed lonely without her but I made up for it all by practicing a new strategy which I planned to apply when she returned. It was all a guessing game as to when that would be but I survived quite comfortably without her even though I missed her blond presence quite a bit. Also during a short period of that Summer I thought of Annie and how unlike Elaine that Annie was. Annie would never have gone away in the first place, I thought. But as the Summer heat rolled in I thought less of Annie and less of Elaine. The time had come for a change and I was ready for it.

It was not for a long time since I had been in the woods where I headed one day on an early July afternoon when the sun was blazing all over the streets and sidewalks of the city. Going to the woods turned out to be a good idea for I had a great time and the whole trip dispelled the loneliness that I was feeling. I walked through paths I never had seen before and I found a new creek though it was not as wide or deep as the others that flowed through that section of the woods. Nature most definitely has its soothing effect sometimes and this time was one of them. I walked for several hours smoking only two cigarettes the whole time and I felt elated after the walk ended.

A few days later I received a letter from Adrienne who was living far away and I read it slowly as I sipped coffee in the morning. The letter didn't say much but inquired about Elaine and some other people I had ceased to see that Summer. I decided not to write back until August or September. This would give me time to write what I felt would be a pithy letter to Adrienne—something I had not done in years to her and I rejoiced at the thought of saying things to her in that letter that I never spoke to anyone at any time. But I had to wait until the next month at least to answer her letter. It had to be that way.

Those were the times that I knew best. Those times were vivid in my memory, such as when Annie came back to the city from the small town in the central part of Pennsylvania. We were very pleased to see each other again and we both showed it to one another. Arthur came over to Annie's that evening and we had a creative session, with speed of course. The speed always flowed when Arthur was around. His supply seemed inexhaustible and he always had some on him just in case. He turned many friends onto the stuff just as he took many pills himself.

A trip to the museum

A concert at the local college

Victorious Delusions
A Tale of the Late 1960's

A trip to another smaller musuem

A speed session, with Arthur again

George H. and his acid

A good acid trip

Victor E. Navarro, Jr.

PART 2 - REFLECTIONS, 2000

Victor E. Navarro, Jr.

Victorious Delusions
A Tale of the Late 1960's

The Spring of 1967 was showered with all the glitter of life that any Spring could have. The spirit of adventure was evident in that Spring as was the spirit of peacefulness that hung about the air, making everything tranquil though at the same time filled with adventure. I was studying philosophy at the time and doing readings in philosophy at home at night when I was speeding or when I wasn't speeding—it all depended on the day's curriculum.

As the Spring grew older I took more speed than usual and I became entrenched in speed as if the whole world revolved around it. The speed highs were smooth and conveyed a sense of well-being that is never lost even after the speed wears off. On days that I didn't speed I would head for Shadyside to make the scene there. The weather was warm and it made for good scene making. Everyone was out on the streets in those days. The streets would be filled with hippies just hanging out.

SPEED DAYS

The days were getting warmer as Summer got closer. I remember the times I had thirty-five years ago in 1967 when we used to hang out at the Loaves and Fishes. In May of 1967 I took speed a lot and there was hardly a day that went by that I was not speeding. My dexedrine supply was running so low that I stopped giving them out to other speeders. I had taken a lot of speed during the Spring of that year. At times I would speed for days at a time, never stopping, dropping more and more capsules of the stuff as I sped through the nights and days of that most glorious Spring of 1967. It was early May and I had stopped seeing Annie and begun to loaf at Carnegie Tech (now called Carnegie Mellon University). There were trips on acid in between the speed. I once had a bad trip with George H. downtown—we had decided to trip downtown that night. After the bad trip I didn't take any more acid and I again reverted to speed, my first love amid the myriad of drugs to take back in those days. There were also downers as well as speed to take but I preferred speed to the calming downers that were so common among the hippies. This summarizes (generally) the old speed days of 1967. (I took speed a little bit in 1968 and discontinued it after that entirely.)

That there were times which equaled the sixties in adventure is not to be doubted. But the sixties were filled with eras of adventure in their whole atmosphere of festive occasions. The sixties never dampened and continued with the theme began in the Winter of 1967 which elevated the hippie to the starring role of those times. I was alone during 1966 before the onslaught of the hippie and was myself in need of a big change. There were times when in 1966 I would smoke grass in the Summer but they were rare and I really wasn't into it much in those days. The real change came about in the Winter of 1967 when I was introduced to speed by Arthur R. Arthur's mother had a bottle of Estratonal and he dipped into them quite frequently during the Winter of 1967. Arthur turned me on after to the speed and

I developed a liking for it. It helped me write and I did a lot of writing at night while on speed. The Estratonal really bombed me out at first and then it smoothed out into nice highs which occupied the entire winter for me. It was very cold that winter and the speed warmed me in such a way that I took it about once a week during that winter. Towards March I took it less often and then in late March I got my own bottles of speed which I dipped into heavily in April and May. That Spring saw me taking speed twice a week and I enjoyed every minute of it.

The sixties are the focal point for all of the eras of my life. In the sixties there were eras of great happiness for me and eras of great truth and reality. There was the speed era, the acid era, the painting era, the Karen era, the Baba era, the Rosemary era, the Marilyn era, and the Ed R. era. The Summer of 1967 is an overloaded time for me. I have overloaded it in my writings but it was a time of peace and fulfillment. I went to Ocean City in the early Summer of 1967. Jim D. was my constant companion that summer and I didn't take speed or acid much that summer but blended in with the warmth and the greenery so well that I didn't need drugs to sustain me. I read most of Hermann Hesse's novels that summer and was into Zen and Buddhism a lot. Hesse's JOURNEY TO THE EAST inspired me, as did SIDDARTHA.

In the realm of lost days all things converge to a point in the memory. Hidden from view these lost days come forward at odd times and make themselves known to me at forgotten crossroads of the past. A new beginning can come from the lost days and can make itself felt in the new era that one is emerging towards. This new era shall be an era like no other, an era of unmatched creativity which springs from the past eras as smoothly as a stream flows down a hillside to the valley beneath it. The lost days account of themselves quite well in this transition to a new era. The past brings with it a twinge of regret that can only be removed by a great and glorious reception of the new era, a reception which brings with it certain high points which highlight the new era and give it an individuality with which it can be made. The composition of the era can be said to be "smooth" when all is laid bare and the past interacts with the present in such a way as to give credence to the new era and foster it in a special way. This new era can contain any element that is pleasing to oneself and can begin at any time (usually at the strangest times when things seem suspended in air like a balloon.) The creativity of the new era will be proportionate to the beginning of that era. That is, the new era will be only as creative as it is at its onset, as it emerges and takes over, consuming the time of the person involved and giving breath to the ideals contained in the exploratory nature of the era. For instance, a new era of going to the zoo will have a certain freshness at the onset of the era that will give it a spur towards greater achievement and productivity. Many new eras have come and gone in my life but the predominant feature of the eras has been their elasticity and their endurable qualities. All eras endure in the memory. It is these eras which give life its beauty. The eras are sometimes intertwined with nature, but not always. Nature can give an era a fresh quality especially if it is in the Spring or Summer. Spring and Summer sometimes take the era out of doors and enhance the natural quality of the era.

"You can't tell Elaine anything. She's going to do it or she's not." Mr. Kuput hesitated, not liking to be critical of anyone. "She is a wonderful woman, though, and she knows much about life. Perhaps you don't see her that way, but I found it to be true of her early on in our friendship."

The maid served the tea and cakes for us and I had a sense of warning that Mr. Kuput was to show me some of his knowledge of Elaine, the idea of which struck me as a revelation from Mr. Kuput that he would have preferred to keep from me had I not been in such a depressed state when I entered his apartment. He saw how down I was and surely wanted to jolt me with something which would ease my suffering not only about Elaine but about the way everything else in my life was also going.

Mr. Kuput's voice was like that of an angel from heaven that night and I soon snapped out of my inner doldrums and became talkative though not of the subject of Elaine. It was almost as if I had completely dislodged her from my memory and was content with just being at Mr. Kuput's apartment. I left as a happy man, the sullen face gone as opposed to when I entered and greeted Mr. Kuput with that so common long face of mine; something which I had begun to despise about myself for I had always despised it in others, especially those stone faces on the bus that so frequently occurred even on a bright, warm day in May. "I'll see you soon," I had said to Mr. Kuput upon leaving. I made my way down the long entrance walk to the bus stop (my favorite one it had become) and lit a smoke.

I wasn't thinking about her at all and I noticed a pretty jogger pass by who said "hi" to me. She was tall and muscular, especially from the waist down and I liked her a lot, the little I had seen. I thought how I would like to have met her and talked. Do such things ever happen except in rare dreams where an obscure and strange lover comes upon us by surprise and reveals secrets we never believed could be known by anyone in our city or even country.

I had always looked to India for spiritual truths and guidance. Perhaps it was right here, I thought, right here with that girl who ran by me; perhaps the "hi" was my mantra for an entrance into facts I sought. Besides, her flesh would have soothed me almost as much as a raising of consciousness.

I took the bus home and had a cup of coffee and tried to read from a novel but couldn't. It was still early so I wrote a letter to a friend in Wyoming and smoked and went to bed in spite of the fact that it was not nearly my usual bedtime but I was so relaxed that I looked forward to just lying in a sleeping position in bed and thinking about the jogger. After all, she was as pretty as Elaine. As I lay in bed I had the realization that I was becoming more free, moving away from Elaine and the problems her madness had caused me, and moving toward something or someone new that would give me a more complete outlook on others, on myself.

Annie came and went but she, unlike the others, has remained completely intact both in my memory and in my romantic notions for her. She couldn't be replaced; but she could be upstaged by, perhaps, a better performer than she had shown me to be back in the turbulent and romantic sixties. Since those times romance has drifted with the sand as from an Atlantic City beachhead so that little bits of passion now and then decrease the awe of that first night on the hillside overlooking the freak coffee house where Annie and I had spent the evening sipping coffee and listening to an amateur jug band, made up of freaks and boppers (mostly boppers) who had joined together to freak out the fourteen-year-old chicks who came every Saturday night.

Annie was all to me in the sexual arena of life back in 1967; Spring, that is, the Spring of no dreams, only realities. This was and has been the way I like it to be. Warm days in April and May and all Annie and me, only Annie and me. My aunt liked Annie and Annie liked my aunt and was nice to her. Forgotten not at all are those days of soft warmth and the heat of Annie in my grasp more than once, more than twenty times. Let's say it was golden sunshine and speed and sex. That about sums it up in one sentence.

Annie brought out the reality of life and those times in the sixties when so much tried to deride and dissipate the creative in the Italian and German, which I and Annie were, respectively.

What a contrast between Annie and Elaine—what a dreadful contrast! As I look on them both I see Annie in light and Elaine in darkness. But of course, the night can have its charms, especially in well-lit, sun-like places like college campus snack bars. Crazy Bob would know (or would have known) that the night can give to one who follows its paths and lit streets along the way to somewhere, only getting there to find not a girl but a sunny morning.

A sunny morning is not merely an end-point to night but a beginning of more going forth from a depression, coming out of a hole or pit that drills the heart and gives rise to dark paranoias so deep they can get as deep as the soul of a person like me or Crazy Bob. Perhaps Mr. Kuput would not know such a feeling or such a depression and paranoia but Crazy Bob would know it to the hilt, to the apex of its conclusion—if conclusions ever really end.

I doubt that Annie was aware of our predicament together but I felt it from early on in our affair. I felt sadness for Annie but also for myself— being a Dago and a Wop. I couldn't live it down knowing what I was, not to others who were not like me, but to myself. I was as lost as Annie was. The two of us together got the same looks from people as I did while alone.

I didn't love Annie at all; but I loved the sex with her, and there was a lot of it with her. I remember it even to this day: it was so often and so sexual, so cool. She was my fuck, my own trustworthy, sexy fuck.

Victorious Delusions
A Tale of the Late 1960's

The question about Annie that still plagues me to this day is whether or not she was a lost soul. Or perhaps **is** she a lost soul now. She was headed for something bad. That is what I picked up then and what I see fairly clearly these days when I look back on the sixties and when I see what Annie was (I see it objectively now; and apart from myself), she seems to be doomed as I envision myself to be now, but definitely did not then. Perhaps I am scared because I was not doomed then, or perhaps my damnation didn't occur until after the sixties. Annie was Germanic, Aryan (as I now see myself to be Aryan) and I am scared for Annie and me that we both may be in the other place instead of the place made for the "chosen." "Chosen" shouldn't be in quotes (as I write this I see my alienation from God and reality), but should be spelled out CHOSEN.

That Annie was a greater love of mine than Elaine, a Jew, is true. I realize it more each day to be true. It shocks me sometimes about how sure we seem to be about someone can change drastically from the actual time of the affair to our older selves which have replaced the younger selves so much and so surely.

Annie went on to follow Baba (a guru) as I also did, but in a different way from each other so that we didn't fuck very often any more. I missed the fucking more than I missed Annie back then in Baba's heyday. But since Annie the person, Annie the good-looking, nice gal I knew many years ago I love so much as to doom myself along with her (though this is not how we are doomed; being a Dago I'm just plain a loser, doomed-devil). As Billy Graham would say, we have been condemned by God (or at least by Graham); so much so condemned that I can't defend myself against the power of the chosen—they are so lucky—at least that luck seems to be the reason which I have trouble believing but which looks more and more to be true.

Annie, come back! Oh I wish for that fuck again, this time with love in it—lots of love. Often I wonder if she feels the same way now about me.

The illusions surrounding and caused by Annie were in total my own illusions, but at the time I thought it was a combination which caused them: in other words, Annie, LSD, and speed. Speeding while on acid and being with Annie who was on the drugs also gave me quite an illusory picture of Annie and reality in general. Reality was distorted to such an extent that I saw Annie beautiful to look at, a goddess in fact and in the fictions I believed then, to be the truth about her. She had a body that wouldn't quit but a girlish manner about her; a naïve goddess, to be truthful; in fact, she was naïve to the point of ridiculousness.

From the time I lost Annie to the time I found Elaine was almost a decade and I believe now I was hoodwinked by Elaine only, of the two of them. Annie seems to me now to have been more sincere, more for real, than Elaine was. Annie's delusions however were much worse and much more intense than Elaine's. A filter could be used to understand Elaine, but not so with Annie. Annie totally lived her delusions to the hilt, while Elaine feigned much of hers and was much more secretive with me and my inquiries to her about the delusions than was Annie.

I was less intense with Annie; more relaxed with her and much more at peace with myself during the time Annie and I were together. There seems now to be no vestige of Elaine, yet a clear and accurate memory of those emotional times with Annie, which were all the times with her to the point of animal energy and attraction. Just as animals fuck and go, that was Annie and I. What fuckings we gave each other? In and out on a nightly basis on speed and acid trips. Coming and going to and from each other, Annie and I were a couple, an integral couple.

I realized years after Annie's and even Elaine's departures how much I missed Annie and how much she meant to me back in those days. How could I have ever doubted her goodness or suspected Annie for a moment? Elaine was so pure in my mind for so long that the impressions she made on me lived years beyond her actual presence and her purity sexually was accepted by me as a great thing, whereas later (much later, it seemed) I saw the failing of such an outlook, of the way she was; and as a person she had lacked the substance of an Annie to the extent that my rejection of Elaine came swiftly to my beliefs about people in general and people all over existence. Annie's substance could never have been questioned if I would have continued with her in the flesh into the seventies; but because of her quick and (now as I look back) surprising exit from my scene of 1969 I tended to lessen her effect on me then though now I know how great it was.

Elaine was full of promises, while Annie delivered. Elaine had class; Annie a body. Elaine was spoiled; Annie never had a nickel growing up. But both came in and out with the wind—Elaine for a Winter; Annie for a Spring. Such is the kindness of Annie that she threw me out of her apartment one night for kissing a Jewish girl. Who can really tell? I can never it seems figure out either one of them. I'm at times aghast at both of them, let alone them singly. But to fight on is what I <u>must and hopefully can do.</u>

What Mr. Kuput saw about Elaine was far beyond my grasp back then. He told me later of her "touch of insincerity" and then I saw what he had seen; the lonely figure of a gal gone phony, especially when she was in his and my company.

Who was Mr. Kuput? He was, in my eyes then and now, the inimitable Jeeves mixed-in with a cool cat artist and, especially, an unflappable gentleman; not of the English variety but much more ethnic, much more dazzling and analytical than an English man. Who can tell me now that he was a phony, perhaps even gay? Such things could never be truly said about Mr. Kuput. Mr. Kuput was the essence of excellence, the crown always correctly worn upon his head; the last resort for down and outers like me and perhaps Elaine.

Mr. Kuput showed a glance of surprise towards me. "How do you like it, Vick?" I couldn't follow. "My painting, Vick." This was a quick rejoinder of remarks I hadn't made. "I think it's tremendous," I told him. "But not on a level with your last one." He added quickly, a retort that started me into realizing right then that I was a decent painter in oils. "Oils are the thing, Vick. They still are tops." He was telling me in such a way that I could have hugged him. It was just the type of thing I had been into thinking about the past few days while randomly meditating upon my art. Mr. Kuput knew the advantages of working in oil versus acrylic and watercolor. He was right on my wavelength like he had been so often over the years I had known him. Mr. Kuput had a way of speaking that would appear to a stranger very unusual but to me it was pure music, his voice and manner of speech.

Mr. Kuput was never dull, or at a loss. Like Ulysses he conquered and won victories many times, so many times that they all couldn't possibly be recollected either by him or by an observer who saw these winnings pass by, sometimes so quickly that it seemed unreal, incredible because they were so decisive and so clearly drawn by him as if the way he accomplished victories of this or that sort was effortless in word or in deed. Mr. Kuput loved to win, the gentle soul that he appeared always to be. He won over an opponent while inflicting no pain as in akiddo, his blows just meant to peacefully disarm his adversary. He loved the struggle with words, the intricate interplay of dialogue and criticism, of contrivance and realism. He never had to admit defeat and rarely did he have to admit that he was wrong; so sharp was his intellect, so concise and at the mark, dead right on the mark. He was, in short, an amazing person. So nice he was while disproving someone's argument or criticism which he felt was unfair or not carefully thought-out. He was always the proper gentleman, even in verbal battle and to such an extent the proper gentleman that even the most audacious foe would gracefully bend towards Mr. Kuput's argument as if he were entranced if not by the pithy commentary then by the exacting but so graceful manner. Many went away in awe of him as many also went away not merely in awe but convinced of a new viewpoint that they had either never thought of or that they had put aside years ago as untenable only to see in a new light the real enlightening strength of that discarded way or idea, the new life breathed into an old pattern so as to become real once again with a slightly modified flavor. Ideas were Mr. Kuput's domain and no one tread those waters more fully and more effortlessly than Mr. Kuput did. Sink or swim you would have to admit upon hearing his discourse about this or that that he was indeed the ultimate intellect you had only thought existed in authors you had read but never met—the real thing in person!

How small Annie seemed to be compared to so many others for so long in my mind and heart until I saw her emerge after years gone by, immense in my comparative memories of the others, including Elaine! It occurred in time that no one had the stature of Annie except possibly Crazy Bob and more recently, Mr. Kuput. Annie celebrated her delusive victories (which were to her at any rate large winnings which gave her art such personal meanings as to appear contrived to the point of asininity).

It wasn't then that her art meant all that much to her but rather she hoped it could deliver her from the delusions that plagued her soul during those times if not perhaps from her childhood as well—for this part of her I didn't know, and still know nothing about, and the results of her delusions when I knew her could never reveal her past before my arrival in those 60s which were so pervasive to us that we (including my own self just as much as those like Annie) were swept up in some storm of the times and those times only; not some delusion of what to some others was real. The bad side of this story was that some persons delighted in Annie's downfall just as they delighted that Annie and I didn't continue together so that the cap would be put on Annie's bottle, her mind gone as I left her behind as well.

Annie's emergence as a factor in my personal history came about gradually as I fell farther and farther apart from Elaine and became more reflective about people I had known. I judged current social associations by those people of the past, long gone except in traces and bursts of pure memory. I compared the current ones to Annie, Elaine and Crazy Bob, as well as others who flowered now and then in my memory like buds in Spring and early Summer.

Mr. Kuput's knowledge in so many fields of the arts and literature was so amazing and exciting that anyone who had dabbled in those areas would be enchanted by Mr. Kuput's talks about such things and even his cordial conversation where he would dip into topics as diverse as philosophy and sculpture as well as the Russian novel and British Romantic poetry. He was never abrasive towards anyone, as I saw it, and went out of his way not to talk down to the less informed. His knowledge and manner flowed from his voice in harmony with a much less provocative outpouring than most professors and creative artists one could come across. He did not <u>try</u> to be nice; he <u>was</u> nice. Of course, to those to those he knew well (like myself and Elaine) he would be more familiar in tone and attitude, but to all he emitted a warmth of genuine delight in talking to them; even when it meant putting up with relentless nonsense and stupidity in some diehards who would not abandon a point of view which any learned person would see as absurd. One thing the intelligent have in common is their unemotional sureness of what they say and the creditable way they say it and explain it to others, even others whom they feel are on the same level. Mr. Kuput's level was high if not the highest and his command of subject matter not lacking in any discipline which he introduced into the talking sessions. I had heard him many times back up his beliefs about literary works with an understanding that showed immense study of world literature and careful years of thought of both the classics and moderns in that genre.

Mr. Kuput had a deep voice but was a bit scratchy at times when he spoke carefully and more slowly than his usual way of talking. Of course, being a writer made him want to speak as he wrote; which was clearly and, at times, carefully so as not to miss a word of his thought which was being verbalized as he thought for he never seemed to think things; rather those important things he said were extemporaneous from his mind directly, without the slightest hesitation, to his vocal mechanisms to the ears of his listeners. This is probably why he had such an acute and astounding effect on his listeners and fellow conversationalists.

Mr. Kuput was alone quite a bit each day, except for visits from me or visits to my studio apartment—a "studio" it was with my homemade easel towards one side with a still undried painting in progress (always in oil). But my real project in those days was to become a novelist; not a novelist of note, but a published writer of quality novels written in a style which I felt to be good enough to leave an air of structure and coherence that would be real writing.

All along in my novels of the spirit and mind I tried to compose what would endure whether I endured or not, not the statements of a death throes by a non-survivor of God's plans for his chosen ones; but as a pure statement of what life and God meant to me, just to me.

Elaine had all but vanished from my desires and even my memories. What replaced her was a creative urge that can be seen in so many artists and writers (of the past, especially; since modern- day writers are so calculating and topically oriented for the big payoff on their books).

Whereas now I believe at the core of life lies "the losers and the other strangers," back then I just looked upon this state of things as just one formulation, a possibility among so many others. Even this is doubtful to me at times, but I continue to return to it whereas back in those days of Elaine and Mr. Kuput (even into the exclusion of Elaine in my thoughts) I put it aside as some kind of madness within myself—reality was different from that scenario, I believed; and I was at more peace with that conclusion at hand, temporary though it turned out to be.

"Well, the Spring days are bringing out the aggressive in me, as they usually do each year now that I've aged and am more stable in my hatreds." Mr. Kuput had a sneaky smile as I saw him walking down the street. "You might say we ran into each other." He was in a mood that he often took on walks, especially on warm mornings; and it was a mood that also made (in such weather) me scheme and plot against my mortal enemies. I told him so that morning. "Great, my boy," he replied with a pat on my shoulder and off he went, agreeing to meet that evening at his place.

It seemed to Mr. Kuput that all the past, his past, had drowned in an energy-field of memories, interconnected yet randomly processed by his brain so that there was no picture of a reality that was once seen and known. "This must be true of others my age also," he mused as he entered his suite after a day at his publisher's office, a day which included lunch downtown at what you would call a "fashionable place." He had some business, important to him, at any rate, to discuss with his publisher, who had, incidentally, published his last two books on the city's arts scene. The second of those two books turned out to be a big seller for Mr. Kuput, at least by his own standards; which, like his personality, reflected a humility without pride.

Mr. Kuput went it alone well, he told me later over dinner. He transcribed some rare art criticism for an article in a local art magazine; or should I call it an art "publication" as those nose-in –the –air arts center people call it; they don't prefer to have it called that; they <u>want</u> it called that. The arts center is filled with these experts to the point that they almost reside there in the galleries. I used to use the facilities there when I was on the streets; but so much for that because it just doesn't fit into the entire opus I hope to record about me, Elaine, and especially the inimitable Mr. Kuput, a man who could <u>never-ever</u> be the victim of a tragedy—he was much too forceful a personality and such a strong, big tall fellow you rarely see in men of his age and especially those types of men of his rare intelligence and knowledge about so much of art and life.

Was Mr. Kuput ever at a loss for commentary? He knew about the practicalities of life very well and he knew art and history to the point that when he spoke, a variety of lights emanated from his face and eyes, and within this context his voice sounded like a pronouncement from God—it was so uncanny! I hope this describes Mr. Kuput as clearly as possible.

Going back to Annie, how I came to see Annie's delusions about herself was rather odd at the time to me and at first I was unconvinced of my theories about her downfall. I felt quite a bit for Annie, just as I felt years later for Elaine. There are times when things of an earlier past repeat the times of a later past. As I see it now I was probably correct at the conclusions I made then about Annie. She became suspicious of those she knew unless she had always been untrusting towards those persons with whom she associated socially, and her roommates who always thought her to be "bananas" as they would say often about her.

Elaine's departure was no shock to me though it was to some extent surprising to Mr. Kuput. His reluctance to accept that Elaine had left for good cheered my sagged spirits about the whole Elaine thing, though I could feel in him pessimism about me and Elaine ever getting back again with each other. His perceptions were exceptionally astute.

Mr. Kuput knew about Elaine's growing delusions of grandeur regarding herself and her role in life <u>itself</u>.

I also was aware of her lapses into these delusions and having hoped they would dissipate was disconcerted when they continued. I saw it all happen to her even though I, too, was a part of it, and I felt guilty as she descended into her delusive state.

One sunny afternoon in June, Elaine came forward to me with the truth about us. She was honest when she told me it was "never gonna be." Now I know this to be true. We were "star-crossed lovers," so to speak. But in the end of it all I gave place to her in memory; a space allotted to her for at least <u>some</u> time's sake, if not for all time.

Often Elaine would mentally "curl-up" and go deeply into herself as if she were hiding in the open stacks of the library and poring into book after book. Although I had actually, literally done such a thing at the library, I was not hiding from anyone or anything and I was not buried into myself as Elaine would get when her delusions became too much for her. She would in the end become paranoid out of nowhere, for no apparent reason, except possibly from misfiring in her brain circuits or some misfunctioning of the chemicals secreted and released in her body which affected her brain in a way that rendered her helpless and paranoid for stretches of time lasting from a few hours to several days.

* * *

How the Fall brings out its colors in the realm of the mind and memory! I remember times that are long gone but still remain hidden in my memory as cliches too readily forgotten but resembling the time vestiges of things long ago realized and given their impetus from long-term fantasies and forgotten days when people like Ellen used to inhabit the stage and penetrate into my life like a knife penetrates the skin when it accidentally cuts it. Supposing all of these things to be true I venture forward in time to the places where I used to roam about and loaf and where I would undertake to systematize my philosophy (of the time) and reorganize my structured thinking along the lines of a new vocation. Everything is blest by this structure and everything performs to a beat of the past; a long, arduous test that makes itself felt in all aspects of life as it contributes to the color of the season in question (which, in this case, is Autumn). I remember Ellen so well (though she is gone now) that I don't even have to go to those special places to recall her in all her reminiscent glory. Those were the times in the drug days when things were so free and easy that you didn't have to plan anything but there would always be something to do, somewhere to go, and something to dream about. Where is there in literature some past that ought to be done over again? Nowhere.

There were times when Mr. Kuput would bring up in conversation with me the topic of Elaine's disappearing years go. I didn't upbraid him for doing this because of the astuteness of his comments about Elaine and his opinions about her sudden expulsion from our lives. Did she look the same now? Or had she changed into a monstress, like a new bride for her love, Frankenstein; not toward any romance but just to be a fitting bride for that awful monster, as he returned from the depths of the collapse and fire of the old mansion on the hill where he was created by that mad doctor, Victor F., who was at the time, very well-known in the environs of his castle of a mansion on the lonesome hill away from the rest of the world's realities; just as he had retired from reality to partake of the noble fields of science and medicine.

Had there been anything behind Elaine's being ousted from our own realities that myself and Mr. Kuput did so well at living out day by day with or without Elaine's presence? Mr.Kuput ventured often that Elaine was, as he put it so concisely, "a sad case." I felt the same way about it all except I had by then lost all affection for her and could not remember what is was about her supposed beauty that had attracted me so much to her in the first place.

Elaine had left. It resulted in just myself and Mr. Kuput continuing our old ways of conversation and criticizing art and music. Mr. Kuput thought the new music mostly poor in quality and I agreed. A rare good music had emerged from the 70s onward into the new century. As for fine art, Mr. Kuput thought most of it silly and contrived (as a joke is contrived from a play on words) and he told me, "art today is rubbish and a bag of lies about reality." That phrase summed up exactly my own opinions though it took Mr.Kuput to put it so well in an actual sentence that I could relate to. He had a way of being pithy without a pedagogical nose-in-the-air manner that so many knowledgeable people exude when giving their opinions about creations.

Mr. Kuput put up some money for me to buy oil paints and art supplies. I thanked him and told him I would see him in a few days. He asked me if I would paint in the meantime and I replied I would attempt to begin an oil but not until I was in the right frame of mind. I went to the art store and got all the supplies I would need to perhaps begin a career for myself; perhaps Mr. Kuput would help me progress with his astute comments about how my oils were (or would be) coming along. I could hardly wait to begin so that I could receive his estimable opinions about my art. "A new career!" I thought. I was filled with expectation of working in oils, which I began as a sophomore in high school years ago at a private school where they had an artist-in-residence who had inspired me to paint.

I brought the art supplies home, which included one medium-sized canvas, wooden at the edges and sides. It was sturdy and big enough to start out painting after so many years of having been away from oils. I was excited.

"The greatest love of all the great loves is the first, Nick." Mr. Kuput was being instructive as well as comforting regarding my recent broodings over the long-gone Annie. "The first great love," he went on, "combines totally the intellect with the dick." Rather than striking me as provocative or humorous, the statement hit me to the core of my soul and made me wonder of Mr. Kuput's own experiences with possibly his own "Annie" many years before I had even known sexual love at all let alone such a type of love I had had with Annie.

"You are too much concerned with a thing to do and to accomplish, Nick." I was struck again just as I was almost shocked at his assessment of great loves. "This art, painting, piano and literature is not necessary to make you into somebody you can feel comfortable with, Nick. You are an integrated person with or without it. You should really concentrate on the philosophy of man and even religion." I was starting to lose track of his argument and I was even becoming slightly annoyed with him for telling me that my painting, piano, and literature were mere cover-ups to my deteriorated self-image. But as there was a pause I realized that he was right, he was seeing the truth about me that I had questioned so often as a mere possibility—but coming from him I saw so clearly now as if it had taken someone I liked so much and whose judgement I trusted implicitly to open up the realm of truth to my own conscious mind. I felt cleansed as I had not felt in many years, since even before Elaine. In fact it took me back to 1967 and Annie and I together when I really had been free of the chain of creativity and was back then really producing great art. This fact I knew all the years since. It was as if those long years were an attempt to jar the fluid of the times with Annie, to recapture her flavor and my own freedom to live and write and paint and play piano creatively to a degree that was so effectively true and real that I was even then in awe of myself and of Annie's influence on my thought and mind-set way, way back in the Spring of 1967.

"Thank you, Mr. Kuput," was what I finally, after much silence, said to him. Was it enough? He seemed pleased at my thanks to his perspicacity. His analysis had been exact to the point of pure truth. I was relieved that he was pleased at my realization of such truth and no longer in the least annoyed by his acute observations of my character and his rounded knowledge of not "just great lore" that we both had had and now I knew something I had never suspected about him. He had once had an itchy penis. And so had I.

"Try a little bit of a pastiche to cover the paint," Mr. Kuput said to me one day while at my studio as he watched diligently as I worked over oils I had already worked into a canvas the day or two before.

His idea of using a pastiche-type effect really worked as I saw it emerge in front of both of us on the canvas. He seemed pleased that I was pleased. "Now you really know oil painting, don't you, master." I told him half-jokingly (at least referring to him as "master"). "Do I?" he replied, half-sheepishly without the slightest trace of egoism though he knew he knew oils <u>so</u> well. "Nick, your strokes are meticulous, <u>and</u> I must say, my ideas work well with your technical skill. Don't you think so, Nick?" "I sure as <u>hell</u> do!" I was siding with him now and he loved it though he was still enthralled at my painting technique. "Such endeavor on canvas I've not seen since my old days studying at the academy." He was pensive now, remembering long ago his own great skills as an oil painter. Skills which, I must say, surely then and even now, far surpassed my own. "Mr. Kuput, you ingratiate me to no end; though I know better to take you seriously when it comes to my painting as compared with your genius at such a thing as oils on canvas." "Now, Nick, don't despair. You are a colorist of unreal proportions. I <u>know</u>. And you should see it unfolding in front of me. I just <u>love</u> your talent, Nick."

I felt uneasy at such humility on his part because I knew how great he was at so <u>many</u> things. The only talent I may have surpassed him in was the piano. And that only because I started at age three while he started at age eleven. My aunt ID had started me on the piano when I was old enough to even begin to grasp the basic essentials of piano technique. She stressed my personal creativity first and foremost and my career owed itself to her lock, stock and pianoforte. ID played beautifully (as everyone said she did who heard her play the piano). She was not limited to classical repertoire either, as I was to become due to my tastes as well as proclivities. She never drilled me or made me learn scales but she did instill in me a love of piano practice, of checking out new and ever more challenging pieces of piano music which she had readily at hand in her voluminous collection, a small portion of which she kept inside the storage compartment of her piano bench. Her black baby-grand piano became a symbol for me of constant reward and pleasure. I loved her and I loved playing piano <u>with</u> her.

I did my painting in two days and tomorrow I would see Mr. Kuput and invite him over to my place to view the completed painting, still very wet with oil and I would be open to his suggestions on what to add and what to change, especially in the details of my realistic work. Realism in oil painting is the most interesting type of art to pursue; even more rewarding than a musical instrument to play well. I played the piano well years ago from this painting excursion but I let it get away from me by not practicing at all for 16 years after I quit the study of piano with Victoria Moderni. She was a great teacher and also a Master of the piano and she dedicated her life to teaching piano at all levels. When I quit taking lessons with her I was an early advanced pianist; just a step or two from being beyond even the late advanced stage of piano technique and I saw an opportunity to begin a career as a novelist. This was my passion at the time though I had written only a few pages of a novel.

Saturday morning was filled with sunlight blasting on my painting, illuminating the colors and especially the details of realistic objects like a lit lamp which I placed in the bottom left-hand corner of the canvas. I applied the paint with a very heavy amount of oil paints to make the details of the lamp stand out. The sun was making it very beautiful and I was then anticipating Mr. Kuput's visit at eleven o' clock that morning. I had bought some breakfast rolls and fresh-squeezed orange juice in plastic glasses; the large sized orange juice because it was so delicious the time I had it during March of the previous year. Of course I had the coffee pot ready for Mr. Kuput loved his coffee as much, I think, as he loved prime rib of beef au jus. I was pleased with the way the oil had turned out. Realism is what I wanted to do with oils and I tried to do the realistic portraits of objects from memory without a study or a copy from which to paint. It was the skill as real as if I had traced it and painted in the color which I never did being obsessed as I was with the natural, the naturalistic, that is, from which I could piece together with brushes the painting I had in mind before I put on any paint to the canvas.

And as the years passed Mr. Kuput and I would still have a social bond, as well as the aesthetic one that had so honed my artistic faculties and judgment. He was already beginning to loom much larger in my mind than even Annie and Elaine. Mr. Kuput had become ultimately my best friend over those otherwise friendless years and I never tired of his intelligence, creativity and especially his kindness.

ABOUT THE AUTHOR

I am a life-long resident of Pittsburgh, Pennsylvania. I attended the University School and was a student at the University of Pittsburgh, where I studied literature and philosophy. I began the study of classical piano at a very young age and have continued composing for and performing on that instrument. My main interests have always been literature and music.

Printed in the United States
23233LVS00003B/4-6